His Wedding Dress

- An LGBTQ+, First Time, Feminization, Short-Read Romance

by Barbara Deloto and Thomas Newgen

To purchase another copy of this book, or to see our other books go to
https://www.amazon.com/Barbara-Deloto/e/B00J21HWA4/

A few of our other books
Realizing Jessica - A Femboy Gets Fem and Discovers Inner Passions and Love
Desires- Fantasy Becomes Reality for an Occasional Crossdresser
Trannies - Two Guys Get Fem
Jessica's Turn: A Gender-Bending LGBT Romance
Frat House - A Gender-Bending LGBT Romance
Finishing School - A Boy Is Sent to a Girls' Finishing School - An LGBT Romance
All Dolled Up: A Student Gets Fem - An LGBT Romance
Sissy Boyfriend
Being Candy
Paying My Dues
Virtual Vacation
Filling in For Her
His New Dress
Her Gift to Him
Telling Her
Feminized to Win
Crossdreaming
Feminized by Her
Taking it for the Team
Feminized Men: A Guide for Increased Joy in Crossdressing
Feminized Vacation
The House of Enchanted Feminization
Heirs to Heiresses
Connected
Our Gift to Each Other
Girlfriend
Insatiable
A New Taste for Life
Spellbound
Femboy Guild

1

My new wife, Janine knocked on the shower door. I could see her petite outline through the steam. "Honey, I'm going downstairs to play some slot machines. Okay, Brook?"

"Yup. Be there as soon as I'm done. Go have fun!"

I finished showering, hurriedly dried my hair, and put it in a ponytail. In the bedroom, I took a pair of jeans and a white button-down shirt and threw them on the bed. Janine's wedding dress she wore last night was hanging there, reminding me how hot she was in it when we had our Vegas wedding ceremony, complete with a drag queen version of Elvis.

I reached out and touched the appliqué of white roses on the breast portion, feeling the satin lining beneath. I sniffed her perfume on it. When she slid onto the bed in that and lifted her legs back, heels in the air, she was so hot in that dress I hardly was able to last a few seconds in her before I embarrassed myself—usually I'm good for at least a few minutes.

I was rock hard, admiring the dress, thinking of her wearing it. I took the veil from the hanger and felt the sheer fabric. It must be something for a woman to wear a wedding dress. I held the veil up to look through it. I placed the comb in my hair. Hmm. Heck, why not? I fluffed the veil over my shoulders and grabbed the dress from the hanger, stepping into it and zipping up the back. I smoothed the short fluffy dress down onto my thighs, feeling the silky, fluffy lining against my skin. My cock was rigid under it. I had to be careful. My heart raced. What was I doing? I reached back to unzip it and take it off. It was stuck.

I sat on the bed, struggling with the zipper. I stood and walked in circles with my hands behind me, one hand over my shoulder and the other under it, trying to reach it better to loosen it. The veil fell over my face. The door latch clunked. Shit! My wife walked in. Her eyes went wide. She covered her mouth with her hand.

"Brook!"

"I thought you went to play slots?"

She picked up her player's card from the dresser. "Forgot this." She put it in her purse and turned back to me.

My heart raced, and my face was hot. My eyes were watery, and I was ready to break out in a sweat. "I'm so sorry, honey. I just had to see how it felt for you to wear this. I just wanted to see. Now the zipper's stuck and I'm so embarrassed. Please don't divorce me!" I heard myself whining to her. "Please!"

She came over to me, lifted the veil from my face, and kissed my cheek. "Oh Brook. I wouldn't divorce you over this. It's cute. I think the reason you came so fast last night was this dress was just too exciting for you. You usually last a couple of minutes at least, and you barely got the tip in and you were squirting."

"I know. I'm sorry about that too. What a way to start a marriage. Just help me get unzipped and we can put all this behind us."

She stepped back, looking me up and down, and fixed the dress around me. She adjusted the shoulders. "Hmm, I just want to get a good look at you in it. I think we're nearly the same size. Hmm, you look cute in it! With a little makeup and hairstyling, you could pull it off."

"Oh honey. No. I don't want to do that."

She looked into my eyes, reached under the dress and her hand wrapped round my cock. "Hmm, seems it's pretty happy right now, even with all that trauma. Maybe we should try making love again. Maybe just like this. You can be the bride. A bride with something very special under her dress."

She wrapped the dress around my cock, leaving the head out. I stared down at it. She stroked it twice and I couldn't hold back. I spewed all over the floor, my knees shaking. "Oh god! Oh Janine, I'm so sorry. Let me clean it up." I pushed her away and ran to get a wet towel and knelt down to clean it up. "There. Fixed." I stood up.

She gave me a peck on the lips and smiled at me.

"Now, can you please unzip me?"

She put a long-painted-nailed finger tip on her lip and tilted her head. "On one condition."

"Anything."

"Anything?"

"What's anything?"

"Anything, Brook. Anything I ask you to do or we leave the room with you like you are."

"Anything. Right, honey. Anything you want."

She unzipped me and I took the dress off and carefully hung it back up, making it neat again and just wanting to keep touching it.

"Brook, it's fine now. Don't worry. It's not like I'm gonna save it for my daughter."

"Right. You can't have children." I carefully adjusted the raised flower petals on the bust. I couldn't stop touching it.

"Brook." She took my hand. "Go put your clothes on and let's go out." She looked me up and down as I stood there naked and limp. "I love how you keep yourself so hairless and smooth."

"I don't have much body hair, thankfully. Would be nice not to have *any*. Except on my head, I mean."

She ran her hand over my chest and kissed me on the lips. "Mmm." She slapped my bottom. "Get dressed. It's time for anything."

I put on my bikini, penis-sheath underwear, bootcut jeans, shirt, lightweight socks and boots. Putting three silver stud earrings in each ear, I then sprayed cologne over my hair and shirt. Adjusting my ponytail, I tied a leather cinch over the elastic. I went back out to the bedroom, where Janine was flipping through her dresses and skirts in the closet. I came up behind her and bent down to give her a kiss on the neck. "Sorry honey. I feel so embarrassed now."

"Don't be." Turning toward me, she put her arms around my neck and gazed up at me. She was five feet tall, and I was only five four, so it wasn't like I was towering over her. She was one of the few women that I looked decent standing next to because of my height. Her eyes glittered like they were full of fun and mischief.

She hugged me. "We've been together since we were little kids and I know you're the one for me forever. I love you. That's why we came out here and got married."

"I know. You're not just my wife and the love of my life, but my best friend too. I just didn't want to make you feel you married some freak."

She gazed up at me lovingly. "You could never be a freak. I love everything about you. I'm happy I caught you with that dress. It tells me more about you. It's exciting. Kinda kinky, kinda what I always thought about you, too. That you're more balanced than other guys. That's why every hunk I went out with or had their cocks in me just fell to the wayside. They could never compare to you."

My face was flushed. I gave her a peck on the lips. "Thanks. That means a lot to me. I just feel bad not being able to be the hunk for you; a guy that can last in bed with you and fill your ever desire."

"Brook. It's a compliment that you come so quickly with me. It means you consider me hot and sexy. Desirable."

"That's cause you are. I watch when we're out together. All the guys have their eyes on you. You could have any guy you wanted. You're one desirable woman."

She grinned. "I am, aren't I? And now that we're married, I'm one hot wife!" She giggled and grasped my hand, tugging me from the room. She yelled in her tiny voice in the hallway as the door slammed behind us. "I'm a hot wife! Woo hoo!"

2

The tension passed through me and all was well again while we ate brunch on the patio by the pool. I couldn't take my eyes off my gorgeous wife. Wife! She was *my* wife. I was *soo* lucky. Even watching her eat a strawberry was delightful. She sat there her sunglasses on, one leg crossed over the other, her one silky leg bouncing over the other in her high wedge heels, the hem of her flowered beige dress just covering her bottom with one manicured hand resting on the edge of it, the cleavage of her firm breasts catching the sun. Her perfume wafted over to me like a kiss. God, what it must feel like to be her.

Janine turned to me as she chewed her strawberry delicately, then she licked those luscious painted lips and her eyes went wide. "I know what I want to do today. Since we'll be here for three weeks, let's start by getting a spa treatment." She opened her purse and took out the literature they gave us when we arrived. "Here it is." She opened a brochure. "The Hedonic spa and salon. All players' club members get thirty percent off. I want a massage, mud-bath, exfoliating scrub down. Then maybe a pedicure, manicure, and haircut with a styling and highlight." She looked up at me beaming a smile and reached her hand over to mine and squeezed it. "Can we?"

"Of course we can. Like you said, anything you want, right? See? I'm good for my word. Besides, we've saved way more than we needed to for this trip and the business is doing well. I'll do the spa with you, then wait for you at the bar." I sipped my coffee.

"Oh good. You remembered. Anything right?" She winked and grinned. She leaned over and gave me a peck.

"Right. Anything." I laughed.

We entered the spa, and they gave us robes to wear and led us to the massage room. It was a private room with two tables and a young man and young woman, both dressed in white medical coats, both good looking and smiling as we entered.

The woman spoke. "If you're uncomfortable with either of us giving you a massage, you can have others to replace us. Or if it should be two men or two women, that too is fine. Right now, the plan is I will massage your husband, Brook, and Manuel will massage Janine. When the massage is over, we'll bring you into a twenty-minute mud bath with an exfoliating scrub followed by a shower and a scented coconut oil and herb bath that will make your body feel electric and your skin like silk. Is that acceptable?"

We looked at each other. Janine's eyes were bright with excitement and she nodded. I smiled at the woman and said, "Sounds great. Let's do it."

We lay down face down on the table and our robes were loosened from our shoulders and folded onto our butts. They drizzled warm scented oil down the center of our spines and their hands began making magic. It was heavenly. It was as if there was an energy coursing through their hands and into our bodies. Janine looked to the side at me, smiling. Her man's gigantic hands were squeezing and pressing her flesh, gliding over her back and shoulders, then down to the top of her butt and under her robe. She rolled her eyes then faced down through the opening on the table. I did the same.

Her hands slid to and fro, teasing my body into submission. I let myself go and closed my eyes, and the world seemed to drift away. I imagined I was above us, watching us both get worked over. Our legs were stretched and molded with expert hands riding all the way up to my crotch and over my butt-cheeks then back up my back, shoulders and neck.

I glanced at Janine. Her hips gleamed from the oil and her rib cage showed her heavy breathing, her breasts pressed into the table.

The woman spoke, "All good? Any discomfort? Are we ready to roll on your backs? You'll be naked unless you want to be covered, but the robes can get in the way."

Janine nodded quickly. I rolled onto my back, my cock sticking straight up. She quickly placed a warm scented towel over my face then drizzled more scented oil down my chest, a few drops falling on my cock as she ran the stream over my legs. She put the bottle down and massaged my legs and feet.

I drifted above us in my imagination once more, watching as the gorgeous hunk of a guy made putty out of my wife with his big hands. Her body shuddered as if she had an orgasm. I heard a little whimper from her. My cock was leaping furiously in the air. I felt the woman's silky hand spread the oil over my hairless cock and balls, barely touching them as she did, making it jump and leap some more. My hips lifted unconsciously, and she continued on to my belly and chest, then arms and shoulders. My breathing was deep. My body was alive with electricity running from head to toe in ripples of waves.

My breathing slowed and my heart rate dropped as the ripples turned into a full body hum that overtook all the other sensations. It was as if my whole body was a cock. I lay there in some sort of bliss. I smelled a floral scent and opened my eyes to see the woman pressing her fingers over my forehead carefully as she smiled down at me. "You're very pretty."

"Thank you. This is heaven. You're very talented."

She nodded and moved from my face to glide her hands down my belly to just above my cock. Her fingertips touched it now and again. Her other hand rolled my balls in her palm in the oil and tugged them. "I'd finish for you, but that's illegal and you'll feel better if you keep it."

I nodded, just lingering in the sensations all over my body with my cock dancing on its own.

Abruptly, soft towels fell onto our bodies, and they wiped us down. They held our robes up and we swung to the side of the table and they helped us put them on. She smiled and said, "Very good! To the mud bath!"

They led us into another room with two tubs of warm, scented mud in them. They helped us slip into it. Next to us, they massaged our bodies under the mud, scrubbing our skin with their hands, exfoliating and sensitizing it. "This will remove all the dead skin that's preventing you from feeling the full sensations your skin can have. Everything that touches it after this will feel special and make it alive."

Their hands roamed our bodies. He spent special time on Janine's breasts and legs. She spent special time on my chest, legs, and cock and balls, though she was careful not to let me come as she gazed into my eyes for cues when she scrubbed my cock and balls with her talented fingers.

They did this for about twenty more minutes and then they helped us up to walk to the shower, where the mud went down the drain and the handheld shower could get it out of every crevice. We went into the next set of tubs for the coconut oil and herb bath, which was almost too hot to go into until we became used to it. Once we slid under the water, the tub's jets turned on and bubbles formed above us. My body was alive and my skin felt like it was being jerked off in silk. Janine lay there looking at me and rolled her eyes. "Heaven!"

I nodded. "Heaven for sure." I leaned back on the pillow. We lay there until they came and got us to rinse off and dress.

Janine took my arm, snuggled me against her, then gave me a peck. "That was a great anything. I'm liking this. What did you think?" She led us out to the mall.

"I thought it was incredible. I even imagined I was floating above us, watching us. It looked like you were enjoying it immensely."

"Oh god. I sure was. His gigantic hands sent this energy through me. My whole body was alive and electric and it felt as if I was having a whole body orgasm but without it ever coming to a peak."

"Me too! I mean..." I leaned down to her and whispered.... "I don't know what a woman's orgasm is like, but it felt as if my body had cock skin all over it the way it was so sensitive. Even now, my jeans feel rough against it and your hand in mine feels like silk."

"It was like that. It was like when a man is deep inside and filling me up and I feel his passion surging through me."

"Like I never can do for you."

"Oh Brook. Stop. I have that anything IOU from you, right? So I can get it anytime I want. Right?"

Did she mean another man? "Uh..."

"You said anything."

"But we did anything."

"Anything means anything... anytime on vacation."

"I see." We walked in silence as Janine stopped and looked at dresses and heels and things. Could I give her another man? I should. My heart raced. My jealousy rose. Then I remembered Manuel and how good he made her feel. Maybe I should hire a full-time masseuse.

"Let's go in."

"I thought you wanted to get your pedicure, manicure, and hair done?"

"Oh, shit!" She looked at her watch. "Eh. That's enough for today. Let's just get some nice lingerie for tonight."

We shopped for lingerie and I was hard the whole time, feeling the fabrics in my sensitive hands and imagining Janine wearing them. She held them up against me as she looked at them, then handed the ones she wanted to keep to me.

She bought stockings and garter belts and waist cinchers and bras and panties and camisole and panty sets. We bought them and they said they could have them washed and pressed and sent to the room in an hour and we left it at that.

"I need a drink," Janine said as she hugged my arm, walking. "Let's get a drink and play some slots on the way back to our room then we can dress for dinner. I'll dress really sexy for you too." She giggled. "And we can go have a delightful meal. Is that good?"

"Sounds wonderful."

We had a martini in the casino lounge amidst the ringing bells and whoops and hollers while we people watched. Janine motioned with her martini to a couple of girls going buy. "Hot outfits here. Anything goes at Vegas. Right, sweetie? There's that word again."

"Yup, anything. What happens in Vegas stays in Vegas. It gives people permission to have fun."

"Exactly! We're gonna have some fun tonight, baby." She pounded down her drink and stood up. "Lets' go get dressed!"

3

Janine and I got back to the room and her new clothes were already there, cleaned and pressed. If you pressed lingerie, that is. She laid out some clothes on the bed and took things from the closet and drawers.

"Let's rinse off together and get dressed. Okay, Brook?"

"Sure."

We stripped and climbed into the shower. The water felt extra special on my skin and Janine grabbed my hard cock and soaped it up, bringing me to the edge while I slid four fingers into her and tried to make her come on my hand.

"Oh Brook, that feels nice. I love the full feeling. Maybe we should buy a toy tonight, too."

"Sure... Why not? Huh, uh..." I humped into her hand.

She let it go. "Not now! Hold it. Don't you dare come!" She whacked my cock with her hand.

"Ouch!"

"Good. I want you to not lose what we paid so much to get today at the spa. Behave yourself."

"Yes, dear."

We dried off. Janine led me to the bed and pointed to an arrangement of clothes. "Put those on before you put your boy clothes on. You'll appreciate the fabrics on your skin."

I looked at her, shocked. "Honey! What if something happens and I break a leg or something? Besides, I'll be self-conscious."

"*Anything*, remember? Would you rather I put you back in my wedding dress and take you to dinner?"

I stared at the clothes. "Right. Okay."

I sat on the bed and started with the pink garter belt and sheer suntan stockings. Janine sat next to me and put on a black satin and lace waist cincher, which took her waist to beyond tiny, and attached her sheer black stockings with lace tops onto it.

I slid the silky sheer and lace pink panties up and tucked my begging cock into them. I put on the slightly padded matching bra and the pink lace camisole over it.

Janine looked at my cock throbbing in the panties. "See how nice that feels, silly?" She slid her breasts into a shelf bra which left the nipples exposed and then slid up a body hugging, thin black dress that barely covered the lace of her stockings, which would show every time she sat. Her tiny feet slid into her tiny, strappy, black, fetishy high-heeled stilettos and set the ankle strap. She stood and perfumed herself and loaded her purse.

I slid on my black bootcut jeans and boots and my black satin shirt and tan suede sport coat. I checked myself in the mirror and sprayed on cologne. Good thing I wore black jeans or my hard cock would show way too obviously.

When I walked across the room, the stockings would tug and slip on my legs, pulling the garterbelt and reminding me what I was wearing. The compression of the bra felt comfortably erotic somehow and wasn't enough to show bumps through the shirt. It was, if not anything else, entertaining.

Janine hung her purse on her shoulder and came over to fluff my curls in my ponytail. "You have such pretty hair with those natural highlights and curls."

"Thanks."

Her eyes flitted around my face. "Hmm." She took my hand and led me into the bathroom. "Just a little."

She took her mascara out and held the wand. "Come here."

"Oh, honey."

"Just a little."

I leaned into her and looked up at the ceiling while she applied the mascara. Then she did eyeliner. Then some lip gloss and then some blush. "There. You look good. See?"

I gazed at myself in the mirror while Janine fluffed my ponytail some more and sprayed hairspray in it. She readjusted it so it was high on my head, then put a black bow in it. "Janine!"

"Shush."

She removed my stud earrings and put in long dangle ones that clinked when my head moved. She wiped off the lip gloss and applied a bright pink 24 four hours glossy lipstick. "Now look at yourself. Nice, huh?"

I rolled my eyes and took myself in. For sure, I looked like a girl. "I look like a flat-chested girl."

"You do! So pretty. One more thing then."

She tugged me by the hand to the dresser and dug out panties and stuffed them into my bra, making me have breasts beneath my shirt. No cleavage, but obvious breasts that looked convincing.

She put bracelets and a necklace on me and some rings, then sprayed me with a sweet perfume. She stood back and looked at me proudly. "Perfect. I knew we should have bought shoes to fit you today. Oh well. Tomorrow we get shoes and gel breast forms so you can have cleavage."

"Honey. This is nuts." I shook my head.

She put her hand on the front of my pants. "Hmm, seems he's liking all of it. If this was repulsive, he'd be asleep. Maybe I'll let you wear my wedding dress soon if you're a good girl." I throbbed under her hand at the thought of it. I whined. "Oh, sweetheart, stop it. You're embarrassing me."

"Oh, stop being embarrassed. You even have a perfect girl's voice, especially when you raise it to whine. Then you sound like a little girl like me." She laughed and pecked me on the lips. "Thank you for being so patient. Let's go to dinner and have a wild anything goes night." She tugged me from the room.

4

"Janine, I feel silly. I mean, I'm a guy and I'm half made up and wearing guys' boots and coat and jeans, yet my face and voice tells people I'm a girl."

"Okay. I get your point. Whadaya say we quickly buy your first pair of high heels and a dress and purse? Then you'd be out of the boy's clothes and you'll feel better... right?"

We stood there by the elevator. I rolled my eyes. "Honey, let me go take this makeup and jewelry off, fix my hair and then go out."

"Go out as a guy?"

"Yeah. I'd like that. I'd be less nervous."

The elevator opened, and a couple stepped out. They both looked me up and down and didn't even pay attention to Janine or her sexy outfit.

I leaned into Janine and whispered. "See? They thought my presentation was off."

"Then let's get you a dress and shoes."

"How about tomorrow? It's been a busy day."

"Okay. Tomorrow. And we'll have your nails done and all of it. Okay? But that's a promise, right?"

"I guess."

I want to make you perfect enough to wear the wedding dress and feel being a bride. Then you can feel how I felt wearing it. Wouldn't that be a wonderful experience for you? You were so interested in it."

I shrugged my shoulders and lowered my head. My face felt flushed. The idea aroused me and I throbbed in my panties. "I guess that might be interesting. You know. To see how it feels to be the bride wearing a wedding dress."

"Good girl. Okay then. Tomorrow. Let's go use some makeup wipes."

We went back to the room, cleaned up my look and went back to a wimpy guy look, and went to dinner. No one paid attention to me on the way, but all the guys practically drooled over Janine. She was my arm Candy.

Dinner was fabulous sitting beside Janine, her hand roaming and rubbing my crotch. My hand caressing her silky stockinged legs. All the while eating and drinking fabulous stuff in a classy restaurant.

Janine whispered, "Relaxed now? Feel better?"

"Mmm, yes. Very nice."

"How do your undies and stockings feel to wear?"

"They're nice against my skin. Much nicer than coarse jeans are."

"Good. I feel really sexy in *my* outfit right now and the thought of you and me being two girls tomorrow night has me terribly excited. So, shall we pay the bill and move on?"

"Sure. Do some slots?"

"Sure."

We made our way into the ringing, clanking, slot machine area and found two quarter machines side by side. We each took a seat. Janine crossed her stockinged legs, revealing the tops of her black lace-top stockings and she bounced one high-heeled foot as she loaded the machine.

We both started playing and soon a waitress took our free drink orders, then quickly got our drinks. We were sipping and playing with spurts of wins poked in with the losses when the person next to Janine left and a handsome tall black man seated himself next to her, smiled, and gave her a hello. He placed his drink on his machine and checked her out while loading the machine up.

He said above the din, "Hi. My names Byron." He held out his big hand. Janine shook it, beaming at him. I could tell she was hot for him. "Hi Byron! So very nice to meet you. I'm Janine!" Her nipples were hard and obvious through her thin dress with her shelf bra. His eyes kept going toward them.

"Nice to meet you, lovely lady. Mind if I seat myself next door?"

"Not at all, handsome." Her foot bounced faster. She glanced at me and raised her eyebrows.

I shrugged. What was she doing? Was she expecting me to like her picking up this guy? I stood up and flung my hand over to him. "Hi. I'm Janine's husband, Brook. We're on our honeymoon."

His big brown eyes went wide, and they flitted around between us nervously. "Uh... hey! Congratulations! Ha ha." He looked around and waved a waitress over. "Get these two a drink on me."

"The drinks are free, sir."

"Oh yeah. Right. They could use another one, though."

She looked at us and we nodded, then she left. He stood and shook our hands again and left.

"What did you do that for, Brook?"

I shrugged. "Jealous I guess."

"I was just flirting a little."

"Yeah, with hard nipples and legs up to your ears. Oops. I'm sorry. We're in Vegas and that's normal."

"Right. Yeesh! You know how many guys I fucked before we moved in together, right?"

"Yeah. So?"

"Don't you think it would be fun for me to have a brief fling in Vegas? Coming over telling him we're on our honeymoon won't help it any. He ran off." She pulled the arm of the bandit mightily.

I pulled on my bandit's arm. We watched them spin. Maybe she was right, but how could I bring myself to let her? My machine hit the payday. It rang like crazy and started counting the payout.

Janine stood, and we watched it climb. People all gathered around us.

It finally stopped at ten thousand dollars. "Woo hoo!" Janine hopped up and down, clapping her hands. The machine spit out a paper. She took it and handed it to me.

I stared at it. "Wow. Ten grand. Guess I was lucky tonight."

She chortled. "Luckier than I was with Byron." She gave me a peck on the cheek. "Let's take care of the money, go get a drink, then go upstairs. I have a plan for tomorrow, and I want us to have some sex and go to sleep so we can get up early."

"Sounds good to me."

We cashed in the stub and had it transferred to our checking account, then went to the bar and watched the crowd go by from the railing seats.

"To being lucky." Janine held her martini glass to me. I clinked it. "To being lucky."

We sipped and watched the couples, the guys hunting girls, the girls hunting guys, the girls hunting girls and the guys hunting guys. Janine rubbed her hand on my thigh. "Nice mix of people, huh? All trying to have a good time. Some really hot girls here. Maybe you'd like to have a fling with one of them. Would you?"

"Uh... You'd do that for me?"

"In an instant. How about it? I'll help set it up for you."

"Uh... not really interested. I mean... girls don't really go for me, anyway. Besides, I have the love of my life." I gave her a peck on the cheek and squeezed her hand.

She kissed me back and smiled. "Well, if you change your mind, this is the trip to do it on. So you're not comfortable with me and another guy, huh? After all the cocks that came in me and I ended up with you, I'd think it's obvious where my commitment is."

"It is. I mean, I know you're committed to me."

"Then what's the problem, sweetie?"

"Uh... guess I'm just weak. Afraid. A sissy."

She nodded. "I understand. It's okay. Maybe tomorrow you'll feel differently about it." She slugged her drink down. "Okay. Let's get to bed." She stood, took my hand, and tugged me up from the seat while I was slogging down the last of my drink. She ran ahead, tugging me, her hard nippled boobs bouncing and leading the way, her hips swaying, her steps tiny in her heels.

In the room she slammed the door behind us and stripped my guy clothes off, then pushed me onto the bed. All I had on were the stockings and things she made me wear underneath. I glided onto the satin sheets and she ran into the bathroom and came back with her bottle of shampoo.

"What's the shampoo for?"

"It's for the same thing I've used it for every time I shower, but I'm not showering right now." She slid onto the bed and slid her legs back, lifted the hem of her dress, and inserted the cylindrical bottle's bulbous cap. She thrusted it slowly in and out while she gazed at me. Almost the entire bottle was going in and out. "Come here, sweetie." She held her arm out for me.

I slid next to her, and she wrapped her arm around me. "Suck my nipples through the dress."

I did. "Mmm, that's wonderful with that fabric on them and your hot, wet mouth. Nibble them some."

I nibbled.

"Mmm, lovely. Come back up here and lie next to me."

I slid back up and her breathing was faster; her legs held back as that big shampoo bottle played hide and seek. "So you like your shampoo bottle?"

"Oh god, yes, why do you think I used the same brand for so long? It's my relief."

"Sorry. Sorry, it couldn't be me."

"Don't be ridiculous. Sometimes I come three or four times a day with it. I'll bet you jerk off, too."

I nodded.

"How often?"

"About the same."

"See? We're the same. We need it. What do you think of when you jerk off?"

"You usually."

"My wedding dress worked well."

"It did."

"Maybe if you're a good girl tomorrow, I'll let you wear it soon. Maybe I'll get another one and we both can wear one and even take vows again. Would that be good?"

I was rock hard and started humping her leg, thinking about it. "That would be really special. So what do you think of when you use your shampoo bottle?"

"Guys like Byron. That's who's making me come right now. I feel him. Of course, a bottle isn't as good, but I can imagine him in me."

"Really? That handsome black guy we just met?"

"Right now it is. It can be a lot of different guys. Sometimes girls too. I could come thinking about you being a girl. Would that be good?"

"I'd love you thinking about me and coming."

"Okay. Well, after we do you up, I'll have sexy images of you as a girl… Mmm…You'll be so sexy. Are you ready to be my bride? My wife?"

I humped on her leg faster. "Oh god yes."

"Good girl. Okay. Right now, Byron is fucking me. Is that permissible, princess?"

I nodded and humped her leg slowly.

"Massage my breasts while he fucks me."

I did her breasts, squeezing the nipples, and she closed her eyes, shoving Byron in and out. Her jaw dropped. Janine bit her lip. She fucked herself fast and hard. She moaned. Her head rolled on her shoulders. God, she was hot. I never saw her so into it. She was gorgeous.

She moved her leg to get me to stop humping it and pushed me away. "Just watch, sister. Watch Byron fuck your wife."

I sat Indian style on the bed, watching her intently. "You're so gorgeous like that."

"Thank you, Byron. Is my pussy nice and tight for you?.............C'mon big boy...is my pussy nice and tight on your big hard cock?"

I lowered my voice. "It sure is, Janine."

"Oh yeah. Breed me. Fill me with your come, Byron." She fucked herself hard and her body shuddered, her head snapped back on her shoulders and she raised her hips. "That's it baby, come inside of me." She shoved it in and held it there while she writhed on it and her body shuddered.

Her eyes opened. She smiled at me. "He fucked me really well, don't you think?"

"He did. You were gorgeous. Incredible."

"Wanna see him fuck me again? He's already hard inside of me."

I nodded.

"Come here and lie next to me."

I slid over to her.

"Take your panties off and give them to me."

She grabbed my cock in her hand, wrapped it in the silky panties. "Now I want you to fuck your panties and only come when he does inside of me. Then we can come together. Something we've never done. Okay?"

"Uh, huh."

"Oh yeah, Byron, that's it. Get hard again and fuck me some more. I love your big, hard cock."

I slowly humped into her silky-pantied hand, being careful not to come. Janine's breath was hot on my neck as I snuggled next to her.

"Oh Byron! Oh god, yes." Janine lifted her hips to him and it felt like she was being fucked right next to me. It was incredibly exciting. She whispered in my ear. "Ready to come, princess? Byron and I are ready."

I whimpered, struggling to hold it back. "God yes."

Her body shook and her legs flung out as Byron went deep. "Fuck Yeah, Byron! I feel you coming in me."

She squeezed my panty wrapped cock in her hand and I fucked it like crazy, spewing my come into them, my body shaking. I had just imagined my wife being fucked by Byron, and she and I both had the best sex of our lives. At least it was for me. I loved coming at the same time with her. It was so connecting.

I hugged her tight to me and whimpered in her shoulder. She stroked my hair and whispered, "Good girl. I love you, my wife. I love you so much."

5

Motors whirred, thick fabrics whooshed and sunlight streamed in the window onto my face. "Rise and shine, sleepyhead." A kiss landed on my cheek. "C'mon. I've been up for two hours already and we have a lot to do today. It's 8AM."

I rolled on my back and she leaned on the bed to give me another kiss on the cheek. A tiny hand made a loud pop as my ass cheek stung. "Owe!"

"Up up, little girl!" She pulled the sheets back all the way and tugged my feet off the bed.

"Okay already. I'm up." I laughed. "You certainly are excited, Janine." I stripped off the garterbelt, stockings, bra and camisole and threw them in the hamper. I stepped into the bathroom and shut the door to sit on the toilet to take a poop.

"Of course I am. I bought you some wedge heels in your size and a pretty floral minidress, so we can go to the spa and you can become the girl of my dreams."

I undid my ponytail, and I stepped into the shower. "I thought I might escape this." I ran a razor over my body and washed my hair.

"Nope. Anything goes. Don't worry, none of the changes are permanent unless you want them to be. We're just cleaning up our looks today."

"Right."

"Oh, by the way, use the shower attachment. You'll love how clean you'll feel after."

I grabbed it in my hand and looked at it. "I thought this was for women."

"And men. It's to clean out your bottom. Do it. You have to. It'll make you feel so clean. Just do it."

"Uh... I don't know. You use it in your bottom?"

"Yes! What if I have two men at once? I need a nice clean place for them. Now do it and see how good it is."

"I'm not having men in me."

"Just do it or you're going downstairs looking like a guy in my wedding dress. This is part of the anything."

The door opened, and she came in. "Do it!"

I did as she instructed as she sat on the counter, watching me through the frosted glass.

"Good girl. Good, huh?"

I took the towel from the door and dried myself. "Not bad, actually. It feels nice and clean." She left the room.

Out of the shower, I saw her wedding dress hanging there again, looking like a work of art. Drying my hair in the mirror it taunted me over my shoulder. I kept glancing at it and as I did; I got hard, and it wasn't thinking about her wearing it, but about how good it felt on me and how good coming in it was. There was no ignoring it.

Janine came back in, placed a makeup kit on the counter, then sat on the counter crossing her legs and bouncing a foot. "I can do your makeup. Your dress has baby blue flowers in it to match your eyes, so baby blue eyeshadow would look nice."

"Really? Do we have to do this?"

"Absolutely."

She opened the makeup kit and began doing my makeup. "Now pay attention. I don't want to do this every day for you. It's ridiculously easy once you know how."

I nodded, and she did my mascara, eyeliner, eyeshadow, thinned my eyebrows with tweezers and lined them in, contoured my face, blush, then lip liner, making my lips fuller, then filled it with twenty-four-hour lipstick. My fresh face was in the mirror. I was a girl with a bare, flat chest. My jaw hung there.

"See? How pretty. You're a *perfect* girl." She played with my hair and put it in a high ponytail. "We don't need to play with your hair or nails because they're all being done." She finished and slapped my bottom. "Go dress. Your things are on the bed, then we can go eat. There's some skin cream to put on too, because it's so dry here. I'm starving."

I went into the bedroom, took some of the floral scented skin cream and did my body, paying a little too much attention to my cock and almost making a mess. Then I sat on the bed and slipped on a pair of beige lace panties and a matching bra that was slightly padded, but too big to not have the cups cave in. I assumed the other panties were to fill the cups and did so.

Stepping into the dress, I adjusted the V-neck, then slid into the wedge heels and strapped them. I stood and went to the dresser and changed my earrings to the ones Janine had left out for me, then sprayed the lovely perfume that was out, under and over me, and loaded my purse. I walked back and forth in the wedge heels. "These are very comfortable."

"Good. We'll be doing lots of walking." She took me to the full-length mirror and hung my purse on my shoulder. "Perfect. Wait until you're redone and we get gel breast forms so you can have cleavage. That dress makes your eyes pop with that blue and the shadow."

"Thanks." I stared at myself. I was better looking than I ever was as a guy. It was weird. I aroused myself as if I was a target of my desires. Luckily, it didn't show because of the flared hem of the cotton mini-dress.

Janine's hand pressed on the front of my dress and rubbed my cock. "Seems you like how you look too, huh?"

I nodded, still in awe of how pretty I was.

"Okay, Brook. I'm a famished girl. Let's go eat and go to the salon."

We had a wonderful breakfast on the patio with the warm breeze flitting up my dress and caressing my bare legs and me throbbing in my panties the whole time. We marched to the lingerie store, and a young lady fitted me for gel breast forms and we bought a few bra and panty sets along with more hosiery and nightclothes, all which we had sent to the rooms except for the forms, which I wore out, thrilled to have such lovely cleavage. It looked as if I had real breasts! It was freaky and fabulous at the same time.

We made our way to the salon and sat side by side facing a wall-length mirror. Girls descended upon us and began working on our toes and fingers while Janine gave instructions to the barber. Soon, my hair was in foils and being highlighted, as was Janine's. Then it was rinsed and wavy curls added with a smelly lotion. Next they snipped away, but our hair didn't get too much shorter other than cleaning up the ends, even though hair covered the floor.

I watched as our new styles took form in the mirror as they dried us with round brushes and a hair dryer. When they were done, I had a layered, highlighted, face-framing cut, with loose bangs in various thickness strands on my forehead. I was as cute as a bunny and very sexy. Janine wore a similar style and was flipping it back and forth, giggling in the mirror.

The stylist beamed at us in the mirror. "It's very easy to care for. Just fluff it anytime and it'll come back to shape." She mussed it with her hands, then fluffed it and it was perfect.

"Wow!" I couldn't help but smile ear to ear. "Thank you, I love it!"

"Thanks. You deserve it. It really shows off your best features." She took the cape off me and brushed me off. I looked down at my pretty little pink metallic toenails that matched my now very long pink metallic fingernails. I admired the perfect job they did on my nails, rotating my hand to capture the light. It made my hands look so feminine and small.

My barber pointed to my hand. "The nail girls are awesome, aren't they? I think they're the best around. They'll last weeks too."

"I hope so. I never want to lose them."

We paid and left, both of us giddy with our new looks. Janine was simply stunning. A tiny, sexy, princess of a wife. I was so damn lucky. "I love your new look, Janine. You are the best wife in the world."

"And so are you. You like your look?"

"I do. It's crazy. I like it much better than the way I looked before all of this. It seems to suit me better. I feel... right."

"Good. Now we just need to get your brain in the right place. Okay. Onward." She looked at her watch. "We're doing good. Okay, Brook. Now we go to where I bought the wedding dress. We'll got one a size larger for you and we'll see what dresses and shoes they have for this evening. I want to take you out to an elegant place for dinner and drinks."

"Really? Wow! I can't wait. I'm getting my own wedding dress?"

"Yes! You've been a really good girl and look at you. You'd make a perfect bride and we could have another ceremony to establish you're a wife. I'd love to see you as a bride taking vows." She stopped us walking and lifted herself to give me a peck on the lips. "My pretty wife."

My heart was racing as we entered the store. I imagined us being married with us both in those incredible wedding dresses, then us consummating our marriage again while we were both wearing them. There it was! The wedding dress on the mannequin with the veil over her face. We approached it and I couldn't help touching the beading and flowers.

A cute young lady came over. "Can I help you ladies?"

Janine nodded. "Yes, we'd like this dress and veil in a size 8."

The girl checked through the rack and shook her head. "Not here in white. We have black, gold, and silver though, less the veil, of course."

My heart sank.

"We can order it, though, and it'll be here in a couple of days if that works."

My eyes popped open. "Perfect! Let's do that."

Janine was flipping through the rack. She held a black dress in the same style up to me. "Your size! You can wear it to dinner tonight and I can wear the gold one. They have it in my size."

"Like to try them on? The changing room is by the counter."

I snatched the one from Janine, and she raced behind me to the changing room. I *had* to put it on. I slipped off the cotton dress and slid into the black one. It had sparkles on it, along with beading and raised black flowered embellishments, exactly like the wedding dress. The V-neck fit my breasts perfectly and my cleavage popped. The off shoulder sleeves fell to a sexy level and stayed comfortably in place with the silicone ribs in them. I looked in the mirror and fluffed the silky, fluffy, crinoline skirt, very short in front and slightly longer in back. I loved it.

Janine held hers, smiling at me, marveling in front of the mirror. "Gonna be a hot time in the old town tonight, baby. You love it, huh, Brook?"

I nodded hurriedly, my eyes wide with excitement. "It's *soo* pretty!" I turned back and forth, admiring it. The teasing, sweeping hemline, the way it showed my legs off, the cleavage it revealed, the detailing of it.

"Super! It looks fabulous for you to wear to an elegant dinner. You still want the wedding dress?"

I turned to her, shocked. I whined, "Of course I do! There's something special about the wedding dress, even though it is the same dress. This dress is beautiful, but it's not a wedding dress. Please!?"

"Of course, princess. We'll get the wedding dress too, then. I'll get this gold one for tonight. I know it fits me. Do you like it? We'll we make a classy couple of ladies tonight in black and gold?" She held it pressed against her stomach.

"Oh god, yes."

"Okay. Get back into your street clothes and we can get you wedding shoes and shoes for this dress and I'll get a pair for my dress. And we'll see what accessories we can get to match too."

I changed, and we were back on the floor handing the salesgirl our dresses. Janine put her dress on the counter. "Now we'd like shoes and accessories to go with the all the dresses if you have any."

"Oh my! Wonderful. We certainly do. Follow me."

We found it all. Titanium, thin stiletto heels, 12 cm high with delicate straps, and thin firm soles in each color we needed. Costume jewelry for wrists, ankles, ears, neck and fingers, and even hair combs to match and finally, fingerless gloves to match our dresses. It was incredible. I couldn't wait to put it all on and see us both in all the finery. We'll be like princesses out of a storybook.

Of course, they would send it all to our room, cleaned and ready to wear. I could live here forever. It was so easy to shop and do things. Then it hit me like a load of bricks. Some day, we had to get back to work. What would I do then? I was living an unreal life masquerading as a woman.

We stopped at an outside bistro for iced coffee and to watch the tourists pass. I crossed a leg and bounced a foot, watching my painted-long-nailed fingers grasping my straw as I sipped the cool, refreshing drink. People milled about escaping work and having fun. Work. Shit. End of the honeymoon. Back to normal. I should have felt good about it, but I didn't.

I gazed off, watching the crowd go by. Janine sat there happy as a clam with what we had done. She turned to me and grasped my hand, then squeezed it on the table. "Penny for your thoughts...young lady." She giggled.

I looked into those pretty eyes full of joy. How could I tell her I was afraid? "I'm such a jerk."

Her face dropped. "Brook? What's the matter, princess?"

I took a deep breath. "I just remembered we have to go back to work and we have to go home and we have to leave this little...

escape... where I play act as a girl and get giddy about dresses." My sunglasses hid my watery eyes as I slurped the last of my iced coffee.

"Oh honey! It never has to end. Why does it? You can be this way forever. I'd love for you to be this way. I've never seen you so happy."

I rolled my eyes and took the glasses off, and dabbed my eyes gently with the back of my knuckle so as not to ruin my makeup. My voice was choppy. "Then why do I feel like such a fool and such a fake? It's because it's all wrong. It's not who I am. I'm a guy, and that's that." I looked around to see no one heard me.

She squeezed my hand and leaned into me. "You are the farthest thing from a guy I know. That's why I love you so much. You're special. You're the perfect balance of male and female and you look your best and feel your best presenting as a girl, and so be it. Be the girl you are and stop this nonsense. Show your courage and face it. Put aside your old paradigms and be the girl you are. We're married. We'll always have each other. Let's enjoy our lives and not hide from who we are. Fuck anyone who thinks otherwise." She threw my hand on the table and leaned back.

She put her sunglasses on to hide her tears while her chest jerked when she breathed. She made little whimpers. It made me feel like a turd. I grabbed her hand and squeezed it. "You're right. Being a baby is all I am. I'm an idiot. I know I'm a girl. I want to be a girl. I always wanted to be a girl. Thank you for showing me who I am."

She took a deep breath and settled down. Sipping her drink, she took her glasses off, dabbed her eyes with her knuckle and put them back on. She gave me a flat smile. "You're just saying that. Then when we get home, you'll revert and be all depressed and I'll have made things worse rather than better. Then we'll fall apart."

"Stop catastrophizing. I won't. I mean it. You're right. I'm wrong. I want to be a girl all the way."

"All the way?"

"Yes. I want to be your wife."

"Okay. I want to believe you. You have to stay this way or you'll live life being miserable. Fuck... I need a drink. You?"

"Sure."

She looked at her watch. "Our clothes should be there in half an hour. Let's get one at the pool patio and relax a little in the shade."

"Okay, honey."

I stood and took her hand in mine, and we strolled. "I love you, Janine."

"I know. I love you too. We had a productive talk. Your words made me feel closer that you're committed and will do anything to convince me."

"I will. Really. I mean what I said. You helped me see it. I was being stupid."

"Good. Because we have two wedding dresses now and it would be a shame to waste them with no grooms around. Being a girl means if you're a bride, there's a groom. Right?"

"Uh... Not always."

"Well, as the pretty girl you are, men will approach and desire you. More than when you were masquerading all your years as a man."

"And I'll send them on their way like I have before. No problem."

"But honey, don't you want to know what it really feels like to be a bride? To have a man longing to make love to you? Think about that dress. I know you like the black one, but you wanted the wedding dress too, and we bought it. What makes that one so special?"

"Uh...it's white?"

"Yes. Virgin white. A wedding dress is a statement of a girl untouched until her husband takes her on her wedding night and fills her with his passionate release. Now that makes the wedding dress different from your black one and you want to experience that, but you won't allow yourself to admit it. You're the virgin bride. You long to be the virgin bride with all the mystique and the thrill of giving yourself to a man. Right?"

I shrugged my shoulders. Was she right? She may be and I'm not recognizing the fact. "Hmm… I see your logic... A wedding dress is a symbol. A statement. It carries a lot of meaning to wear one…. but... hmm."

"Okay then. But I think you'll have to be patient before you can truly wear it and experience what it brings to a person. You need to grow as a young lady and I'll help you if you let me."

"Okay."

"Trust me?"

"Of course."

"Then our rule is on again. Do anything I want. Right?"

"Uh... anything?"

6

We finished our drinks and went back to our rooms. By the time we had gotten there, all I could think of was dressing for dinner. Someone neatly placed all our things on the vast bed. I gasped when I saw it. It was like a work of art, with all the pretty things spread about in order.

Janine grasped my arm and hugged me to her. "Like a work of art, isn't it?"

"I was just thinking that myself. It is."

"Lets' rinse off and get dressed. Wash your face and hair and I'll help you redo your makeup for an evening look. Okay?"

I nodded quickly and took my clothes off in the closet, Janine alongside. She took me by the hand as we stepped naked into the shower.

She shampooed me, and I shampooed her, and we washed each other with loofahs. She used her shampoo bottle to bring her to the edge, then stopped and knelt and sucked my cock to the edge, then stopped. We toweled off and slicked sweet smelling skin cream on each other sensually and slowly, everywhere. We dried our hair, and it was like the stylist said. My hair style all came back perfectly after fluffing it.

Janine and I did our makeup together, and I felt proud at the look I had created with dramatic eyeshadow and contouring and luscious lips. I was hard as a rock seeing myself so beautiful. I felt a cold, wet finger in between my cheeks. "Hey! What's that?"

"Relax and stand still. It's *anything*." I looked at my face in the mirror, my hands on the counter as Janine slid a cone-shaped bulbous object between my cheeks and pressed it against my anus. "No way. Stop."

"Shush. Anything begins here. I'll wear one too."

She pressed it against it and watched my face in the mirror. "Push back, honey. Push back on it until it's in."

My hard cock bumped the counter, and I moved away from it a little and lifted on my toes, then pressed my bottom back against it gently. She looked into my eyes in the mirror. It felt erotic and not bad. Pushing against it harder, it went in further. I pushed again, harder still, and it popped in to the hilt, filling me up. I gasped.

"Okay now?"

I nodded.

How's it feel?

"Erotic. Enticing, actually."

"Good. It's bluetooth. There's an app to download on your phone to turn the vibrator on and adjust it. You can do it later. I'm going to put mine in. Go get dressed."

I walked out to the bedroom; the plug moved deliciously inside of me. Was this her way of getting me ready for a man to be in there? God, what was I doing!? She was going to have a man fuck me. I had to stop this.

7

My remorse over being prepared as a receptacle for men went away when I saw the spread of things on the bed. I stopped for a moment to appreciate how lovely it all was and became engrossed in the task at hand. Finding my dress size, I sat next to it. I stared at it. I caressed it. I touched all the other things. I fondled the dress. My cock leapt and bounced. I had to wear all of this. I just had to.

I wrapped the black lace and satin garter belt around me, clasped it and adjusted it, then slid the gossamer thin stockings up my leg carefully, the sheer fabric sending ripples of pleasure through my legs and into my soul. I attached the six garters to each stocking, making sure to keep them all straight. My pretty little pink toenails glimmered below.

I sat and slid the black-lace, ruffled-edged, crotchless panties up to frame my hairless package, making it look like a bird in a nest. Black-with-pearl garters slid up my legs to rest at the clasps of the garter belt on each leg.

Wrapping the black-lace bra around me, I clasped the three hooks, then turned it to the back, slid my arms through, and adjusted the straps. The weighty gel breast forms were cool against my skin as I stuffed them into the bra and adjusted my cleavage. My leaping cock oozed a drop. I had to be careful, or I'd make a mess.

I unzipped the back of the dress and slid the silky, fluffy lining against my slick stockings and put my arms through the cap drop sleeves and adjusted them, showing the graceful curve of my shoulder. Taking a deep breath, then letting it all out, I tugged the zipper up, snugging the dress tightly about my waist and making it two inches smaller.

The squeeze of the bra and the weight of my breasts and the cinching of the dress leant its own sensual flavor to the delightful picnic I was on. I throbbed and bounced beneath the dress; the tip being teased by the heavenly lining.

Sitting on the bed, the plug pressing deliciously; I slid my pretty, painted-toe-nailed feet through the cage made by the thin black patent and bejeweled straps of the delicate shoe. Poking my toes to the end of the sole, I lifted and contorted my leg to rest beside me on the bed, being careful to not dig the super thin, silver titanium heel into the satin comforter. My painted nails delivered the thin strap to its fake diamond buckle and through it, then found the proper hole and passed it into the buckle again.

I stood carefully in my fetishy high heels and went to the dresser to put on all the matching earrings, necklace, ear cuffs, rings, bracelets and, finally, the delicate fake diamond ankle bracelets.

Janine bought us both some new perfumes, and I took mine and sprayed the intoxicating fragrance under my dress, on my legs and arms, on my wrists and hair, bathing in the stimulating scent. There was something intriguing about it the way it seemed to increase my desires, and my shaft began to lift and fall beneath my dress autonomously.

Taking a deep breath, I loaded my purse with phone, player's card, ID, cash and credit cards, lipstick, blush, hand cream, and a couple of snug fit rubbers in case I felt I was going to lose control at any time. I was so aroused, I needed them just in case it was becoming too much to risk, but I hated to put one on and not be able to feel the freedom I felt right then, being fully erect and free under my fluffy dress.

Wait! My phone. I took it from my purse and opened app store, loaded the app for the plug on it, paired it on bluetooth and adjusted it, going through all the choices and ending up on one that cycled through them all like a repeating playlist of vibrating intensely, mildly, quickly, not at all, vibrating for some time, etc. It sent varying ripples of bliss into my bottom and running through me. I returned the phone to my purse.

Looking into the full-length mirror I saw an image of an elegant, sexy, classy young lady with cupid's bow painted lips, a bow to match the fabric of the dress in the beautifully coifed hairdo, framing a strikingly contoured face, catching eyeshadow and liner, full flirty eyelashes, a luscious creamy cleavage, shapely legs atop sinfully sensual high heels, wearing a feminine, fluffy, revealing minidress, barely long enough to hide my crotch and garters in front and just able to hide my pantied butt in back, wearing matching jewelry all over.

I reached my long painted nailed fingers down to gently and carefully grab my shaft through the dress and give it a few strokes, then let it go to leap beneath it. Not the slightest bit visible. I sat and crossed my legs. Still hidden. I walked back and forth in my heels before the mirror. Not a hint of maleness.

Janine appeared beside me, placing her arm on my bare shoulder, smiling into my eyes in the mirror. "Hello lovely lady. Seems it has captivated you. You didn't even respond when several times I was telling you how lovely you looked. You didn't even seem to notice me."

I realized I hadn't. I took in her visage in the mirror. "Oh god. I am so sorry. I was so immersed in the process and the sensations. You look absolutely fetching. That dress is magical on you. We'll be sending the men away in droves."

She laughed. "We'll see about that." She wrapped our sheer silver sparkling shawls over our purses as they hung on our sides. "In case it's too cold inside."

She smiled at me, happier than I'd ever seen her. "Ready to face the world? How do you feel?" She touched my hair, moving a few strands here and there, her eyes flitting about like a mom checking her daughter before prom.

"Beautiful. Absolutely beautiful. It's as if I'm the epitome of that word in the dictionary. I never really felt handsome, though you have said I was, but I truly feel beautiful right now. So feminine, so pretty, so confident, so sensual, so alluring. Oh, my gosh."

"Do you still want the wedding dress? We can cancel it."

"Bite your tongue. If this one makes me feel this good, I can only imagine how that one will with all of its symbolism."

"Good girl. Clothes make the person, right?"

"They sure do."

"When you have the white one on, you, as a person, will be the bride. You'll have no choice."

That was a frightening thought. No choice. Fate. Free will is an illusion. I took one last look in the mirror. All of it was fabulous even though I never would have chosen this. I pictured myself in the same style wedding dress as the dress I wore. I still wanted it. Maybe she was right about me. Drawing a deep breath, I adjusted my purse on my shoulder, pulled my shoulders back, checked my cleavage, and took Janine's hand in mine. "Destiny is always forward, never back."

Janine kissed my lips gently and touched the back of her hand to my cheek, gazing lovingly into my eyes. "That's my wife talking alright. Good girl."

8

We made our way through the hotel and then the casino to the street. All the while, our plugs running silently inside of us giving a concert of vibrations through our bodies, our heels clicked delightfully, my breasts tugged on my chest, jiggling with each step, my hips took on a natural sway from the tiny minced steps the ultra high heels forced from us by their demands. The fluffy lining of the dress teased my cock as the tip poked against the cloud-like fabric. My skin all over tingled, being no less sensual than my dick.

We held hands and strode tiny strides hand in hand, our chests out and shoulders back, smiling behind our sunglasses as we walked to the Bellagio, a warm breeze threatening to lift our dresses from time to time. All the passersby beamed at us, acknowledging our elegant presentation, the women seeming to wish they were us. The men's warm reception of us on the street spoke of their desires to consume us with their eyes and fuck us with their cocks, getting hard from seeing us go by.

The maitre'd greeted us warmly and led us to our seats at a small booth facing the pond and the water fountain show that ran on and off. The water was just beginning to take on the colors of the lights as the sun set. Lights of the strip behind it added to the depth and scale of the scene.

We slid into the curved booth made for four and snuggled against each other, our silky legs sliding together after we crossed our legs and bounced a foot. We perused the drink menu and found a strong pink floral flavored martini that was delivered with an edible flower floating in it.

Janine held the drink to me. "To my lovely wife. May she become the bride of every girl's dreams."

My fingernails glinted in the light as I held it by the stem and clinked it to Janine's. We looked into each other's eyes as we delicately sniffed the flowery drink and sipped. My eyes went wide with surprise. "If ever a drink tasted like a color, this was it."

Janine nodded. "It does. Totally a baby pink like it looks. Not bubble gum though, but floral pink." She sipped it again delicately. "Mmm…" Her hand glided on my stockinged thigh. She whispered to me in her breathy bedroom voice. "I saw you slip into your crotchless panties. Do you like them? I bet it makes it look feminine and pretty, and I bet it feels incredible under that dress. They make me feel vulnerable and delightfully accessible. I mean, I wouldn't even have to move my panties to the side and someone could put their cock right into me in a second from behind me at the bar. Or take me in an elevator and fill me with their come before I even knew what happened. Or stuff their big hand into me in the theater. Or… Someone could attack you the same way… like this." Her hand and slid up my leg, roamed under my dress, and wrapped around my naked cock, squeezing it gently.

I quickly took her hand away. "Oh god. Please. I'm having enough trouble as it is. It's delicious having your hand there too, but I don't want to make a mess in here. I even brought rubbers in case I felt I'd be out of control."

She giggled. "How cute. I love it. I'll behave then. I wouldn't want you to have to put a rubber on. You could put one on someone else, of course, but not on you and have you miss all the sensations from your pretty dress."

I laughed. "He'd have to be my size. I brought the snug fit ones. Don't think Byron would fit them."

"Byron wouldn't need one. I can tell he'd be clean. Don't worry, I have magnums for any questionable guys."

I rolled my eyes. Sipped my drink.

"Oh, stop being a baby. Once you're a wife, you'll understand what it's like to be filled by a powerful beast, and you'll want it as much as me."

I shrugged and ran my hand over her silky thigh. She caressed mine, and we gazed at the fountain doing its routine and the sun setting behind the buildings. "It's beautiful. Thanks for finding this. It's so elegant and romantic."

"Thanks. This is our honeymoon." She gave me a peck."

The waiter arrived and went through the menu item by item, making it exceedingly difficult to decide. We ended up starting with the chilled seafood platter with oysters, clams and a lobster tail paired with a white Bordeaux.

I wiped my fingertips on my napkin, sensing the coarse linen on my stockinged thigh, relishing every sensation, flavor, and scent. The world was alive with color and taste and fragrances and delicate music while our bodies seemed to radiate energy. I crushed the oyster between my tongue and the roof of my mouth, giving up a kiss of the sea to fill every space in my mouth and deliver it until it entered me.

"How's the plug feel, honey?"

"Strangely wonderful. You have one in and turned on, too?"

"I sure do. See how nice something in your bottom can feel? Just wait until it's a real cock on a passionate man."

As if on cue from Janine, the plug fired off the super intense, pulsing vibration in its playlist, making my leg twitch slightly and my cock leap and it made me wonder if she was right. Would I feel his cock pulsing in me and would it feel even better? My cock throbbed thinking about it.

We finished the plate, and I sniffed my wrist, then sniffed Janine's neck before sniffing the last of the wine.

Janine grinned. "Everything smell okay?"

"Everything smells incredible. Your perfume and my perfume make my cock harden when I smell it. It's as if it had some kind of ability to go directly to that place in the brain and set off the trigger."

She laughed and finished her wine, waving to the waiter. She looked at me, her eyes bright and happy. "That's because these are pheromone perfumes. They have that effect on men. Didn't you see how the waiter grew a hard-on after serving us? I'll bet you can see him twitch under his pants when he's near us."

"Oh god. And I practically took a bath in it. You should have told me."

"Why? That's what it's for. Not that you or I would have any problem making a man hard. But this will attract them more. I wore a perfume like that on our wedding day. It's all over the wedding dress."

"Really? Maybe that's my obsession with it."

"Oh, sweetie, it's deeper than that."

"Does it affect women that way?"

"They make one for men to wear that does. Byron reeked of it. Made me wet smelling him."

"Ah. I see. So I'm like a scented trap for men. Like for deer or rats or beetles."

"Exactly. We both are. They can't help it. It goes straight to the hypothalamus and they become like animals." She giggled. "You'll love it. Just wait."

Janine ordered the next course. I took a deep breath and relaxed, looking at the fountain's display outside and Janine held my hand resting on my stockinged thigh; my cock still hard under my dress. She whispered. "Watch the waiter's crotch. Then later, after dinner, watch what the guys do around us. I can't wait. You'll love it now that you're a girl."

A girl? I opened my purse, took out my lipstick and phone and applied fresh lipstick while looking into the phone. I put them away and, without thinking, I sprayed perfume on my wrist and legs.

"Look at you putting on more pheromones. Good girl, Brook. Now you're thinking and I can see you're ready to grow up and be a big girl." Janine sprayed her perfume on her wrists and thighs.

9

Dinner was more than perfect and we left satisfied and relaxed... except for our raging libidos. "Honey, can we go back to the room before we go out? Maybe we should... maybe I could..."

"No way. I will not have you lose this feeling. We're going out while you're a nymphomaniac and you're going to enjoy it. Immensely." She took her phone out and played with it. "I found a nice dance club." She played with her phone some more. She waved to the waiter and motioned for the check.

The waiter brought the bill, and I paid it on his machine, his cock growing larger in his pants each second while he held his head up, sniffing the air like it was a drug. Janine took my hand and tugged me from the booth. "The Uber's outside."

We ran in our tiny steps, our shawls flying behind us, my breasts tugging, plug singing inside, cock flailing under the silky satin of my dress. The driver smiled and opened the door of the Uber black and we slid in. Once inside, he looked in the mirror. "You ladies look tremendous. Big night, huh?" He pulled away.

Janine smiled at him in the mirror. "Yes, it is. A special night. My husband here is going to learn to please men tonight and I can't wait. I might get laid."

His eyes lit up. I poked her in the side and whispered in her ear. "Janine!"

"We'll never see him again."

He grinned ear to ear. "Your husband is gorgeous like you, ma'am. You'll have no problem getting anything."

Janine laughed. "Yes sir. *Anything*. Right Brook?"

"Right."

He pulled up front and came back to open our door. "Enjoy your evening ladies, and I hope it all works out well. Congratulations to your husband for finding her calling." He winked and nodded at me. His cock was hard in his pants.

Janine stopped outside the place, holding my hand, and looked around. There was a guy just finishing a smoke. He put it in the ashtray and walked away past us. Janine touched his arm. "Could we bum a couple of smokes from you, sir?"

His eyes lit up, and he took the smokes from his shirt pocket, handed each of us one, and lit them for us. Janine touched his hand when he lit hers. His cock was already hard in his jeans.

Janine winked at him. "Thank you so much."

"Anytime ladies. I'd stay and talk, but I'm in a rush to meet a lady." He ran off.

"We smoke now?"

"Why not? You could use it to calm yourself. Right now, I'm also pretty jittery. I feel like a virgin for some reason. I'm so excited for you, I guess. You're going to do girl things with men. Feeling your power from stirring their passion."

"Really? Power?"

"Of course. Ready?" She inhaled a big drag and blew it out through puckered lips. I looked at my lipstick on the filter and throbbed in my panties as the plug hit the big one again and my knee shook from it.

"Uh... not really. I mean...it sounds interesting, but when I think about it, it scares me. I'm a guy in a dress."

"You saw how the driver didn't care. No one cares out here. To any guy, you're just another pretty girl they hope will make them feel good."

"I guess." My heaving breasts reassured me I was a girl as I puffed again. I whispered. "I'm a girl."

"What honey?"

"I said, I'm a girl."

"Good girl. Now let's get this over with so you can prove what a big grown-up girl you really are. Then you'll be the girl for your wedding dress and wear it as you'd want to with all its meaning and flavor."

10

The dance club pounded a primitive, pounding beat. Janine led me by the hand around the club, looking for seats. "There Janine. Right there."

"No, not that one. I want a special seat."

She dragged us around through the mix. The men all sniffed the air around us like dogs that caught the scent of a dog in heat. A large hand would grab a feel of my pantied bottom when we passed some men. Others would try to catch our attention as Janine took us on our mission. Finally, we made it through the gauntlet and slid on either side of a large booth in a dark corner at the back.

The leather seat was cool and refreshing on my sheer pantied bottom when the waitress came over in her skimpy minidress, her nipples showing through her top, and towered above us in her platform, stripper shoes, bending over and giving us a mountain view. Her bimbo voice said, "Drinks, ladies?"

Janine nodded and cupped her hand to yell to her. "Two Dirty martinis and two waters please. Lots of napkins too, please."

The bimbo took off. Janine held her hand out for me to take as I looked across the booth at her. "I love you," she mouthed more than said through the pounding music. I could feel the bass notes in my breasts and cock, they were so solid. I mouthed it back to her and plugged my ears with my fingers, making a face.

She nodded and mouthed, "I know. It won't take long." Pointing to her watch then making a leave sign with her thumb.

I nodded. When I turned to look out at the crowd, there were four cute guys standing there with their drinks, asking Janine something. She nodded and motioned for them to join us and she slid out to let one in, motioning for me to do the same. I slid out and let the somewhat feminine looking one in first and then the larger, taller, more handsome looking one in.

They yelled their names in my ears, and I did the same for them. I crossed my legs under the table, locking my cock between my thighs. The waitress came back and delivered our drinks, and one guy paid for them and ordered another round for all of us.

The guys on my side of the booth were snug against my leg. I could feel the roughness of the big guy's jeans on me and the silky smoothness of the black dress pants of the cute guy. Janine sprayed on more perfume and handed hers to me. I sprayed it on my legs and wrists and some in my hair and on my neck.

Both of the guys seemed to really perk up and their hands ended up caressing my legs and trying to push between them. Shit! I pounded down my martini and looked over at my wife for help. She laughed and already had one guy's hand stuffed in her crotch, while another guy played with her boobs and nibbled her neck.

I locked my legs, put a hand on each guy's crotch, and played with their zippers. I had to distract them from my secret, whether or not Janine thought they'd care. They quickly obliged me by unzipping and unbuckling their pants and pulling out their packages. Before I knew it, something previously unimaginable to me happened. My fingers wrapped around a cute cock and a huge cock, both hairless and silky. The feeling of their hard cocks in my hands didn't repulse me a bit. Their response to me thrilled me. I stroked them with both hands and looked back and forth between them.

They kept trying to get between my legs. Suddenly, Janine disappeared beneath the table with a handful of linen napkins. I looked at my guys and decided that might be the best thing to get some distance from them, grabbed the rest of the napkins, and slid under. Janine had placed some on the ground for her knees and I did the same. She reached over and gave me a quick kiss, yelling in my ear. "Be a big girl and suck those cocks."

I stared up in the dim light at the guys jerking their cocks, waiting for me to do something. If I did nothing, I'm sure they'd just come all over my hair, then leave. I could wait for that. It excited me to think I was making them so hot.

Reaching up, I grasped the cute guy's cock in my one hand and held the other cock in my other, trying to stroke it. I leaned into the little one and stared at it, jerking it between my thumb and forefinger. I moved forward and sniffed. It smelled of a fresh, clean cologne. I rubbed the tip with my thumb, making him twitch, and his hands reached for me under the table.

I pushed his hand back, wrapped my lips around the head and began bobbing my head on it. His hand rested on my head to protect it from hitting the table, and his hips pumped into my face. I ran my tongue around his shaft vigorously while squeezing it with my lips and bobbing my head and rolling his silky balls in my palm. He rewarded me with his legs becoming stiff, his hands squeezing my head tight, and his cock pulsing and shooting thick come in my mouth. I instinctively swallowed what would choke me if I didn't. His reaction to me was a tremendous compliment, making me proud and wanting more.

When he finished fucking my face, his body went limp, and he put himself away. I moved over to the big guy's enormous dick and dove onto it with a fervor I never knew I had for such a thing. I used one hand to stroke the bottom and one hand to roll his balls in my hand while I bobbed and squeezed my lips tight on the top portion of his cock that stretched my mouth to the limit. The residual taste of compliments from the one I just finished drove me to harvest more.

My plug was dancing, going through the playlist and my cock was being teased with each leap it made under my dress, the tip sending ripples of twitches into my body while I consumed and ministered to the incredible cock in my hands and mouth.

I loved the response from him, the way his hips moved and his hands caressed my head, and if I could hear it, I was sure he'd be moaning and calling my name. I wished I could see his face and tried to peek with one eye. He was looking down at me with a longing in his eyes. I knew I was driving him crazy.

Just when I thought he'd come, I stopped and pulled back and his hands flailed around under the table, trying to bring me back. I leaned back and just massaged his hard legs, letting him know there'd be more. When he settled down, I slowly took his cock into my mouth, bit by tortuous bit, barely touching it with my hands or mouth, breathing on it. I flicked the tip with my tongue repeatedly, making him squirm each time. He grabbed my head, and I pulled away, leaving me to admire it bobbing in the air while I massaged his legs.

When he settled down again, I had to harvest my compliment, and I needed it *immediately*. I *dove* onto it with vigor and passion; tugging, rolling, running around it, bobbing, squeezing with my lips, and sucking. His legs tensed, his hands squeezed my head tight and his magnificent cock pulsed in my wide open mouth, spewing endless come into my hungry throat, which I swallowed as if in a beer chugging contest. While his pulsing cock deposited compliments into me, I came like a rocket under my dress and hit my head under the table with my legs shuddering beneath me.

After what seemed a quart of semen and maybe 13 or 14 swellings of that sumptuous cock, I licked it dry and flicked the opening with my tongue until he made me stop. When he settled down and I caught my breath, I took clean napkins with me and slid back up in between the two guys. They both put their arms around me, peppered my cheeks with kisses, eliciting a smile from me that went from ear to ear. While I wiped my own come from my legs and dress, I realized I was immensely proud and gratified and I was so wrong about not doing something like this all these years.

The cute one handed me a fresh drink.

11

Janine sat by herself, the guys gone, fluffing her hair and adjusting her dress. She crossed her legs and lifted her drink, then looked at me and lit up with a huge smile. She yelled, "Good girl! I'm so proud of you!" Her hand came across the table and grabbed mine. "Wasn't that a gas!? Wasn't it wild!? We need to get out of here. It's too damn loud." She finished her drink and reapplied her lipstick, looking in her phone, and it reminded me to do the same.

We slung our purses and shawls and slid out. Janine guided me through the crowd and back out into the peaceful, fresh air. We walked back to our hotel. "So, was it great?"

I laughed. "It was a surprise. It amazed me how good it was. I was so into it and so thrilled by the way they reacted to me that I came all over my dress and stockings."

She snuggled to my arm as we walked, the cool breeze blowing under my dress, cooling my damp, hard, bouncing cock.

"I knew you'd love it, Brook. Is the plug still in?"

"Oh yeah. I'm hard again already."

"Good. Then let's just have another drink at the hotel bar and go to bed. Okay?"

"Sure. It's been a heck of a busy night already. How was your time with them?"

"The usual. I love doing that. It's so much fun driving them crazy."

"I love that part."

"Wait until you get a compliment shoved deep inside your pussy. That's what I didn't get tonight. I didn't come yet."

"We can work on that in the room."

"I guess." Her face had a look of disappointment.

We entered the hotel and went to a quiet but very busy bar and found a couple of plush swivel seats at it and ordered a drink. I crossed my silky legs and bounced a high-heeled foot, as did Janine. I unconsciously took out my perfume and put some on my wrists and neck. Janine took it from me and sprayed herself all over. I could feel the effect beneath my dress and adjusted myself to trap my cock between my thighs in the damp lining.

Our drinks arrived. Janine held hers up. "To both of us, getting laid soon."

I rolled my eyes, clinked, and sipped. "I don't know about that... for me, anyway."

"So you're good with me getting laid?"

"I guess."

"I won't unless it's okay with you. It sounds like you're okay with getting laid now. You toasted to it."

"But I said I don't know about it."

"What don't you know?"

"I mean, it would be in my bottom. You don't have to do that."

"It's good though. It's sometimes better than the front. You'll love it. You love the plug, right?"

I nodded and sipped.

"It's better than that. In order to wear a wedding dress, the bride has to agree to be impregnated. Want to be a bride or not?"

"I do. Really. I know I'm being silly."

"Would it help if you saw me take it there first?"

I shrugged. "You don't have to. You take it anyway you want. It's okay. I'll be there, right?"

"Of course. I wouldn't cheat on you. I want you there with me. I want you to see what a deep connection to a magnificent cock is like for a girl, so you can see what a wonderful gift it is to me and so you can be ready to feel it, too. Will you do that for me? I think it'll help you become a bride yourself once you see how good it can be. You saw me with my shampoo and loved it."

I nodded. "Okay. Yeah, you're right." I throbbed under my dress, thinking about it. "It's exciting for me to think about, actually."

"No jealousy?"

"Nah. Why? We're married and committed to each other. Right?"

She gave me a peck on the lips. "Right."

We sat and relaxed, Janine gliding her tiny hand on my silky thigh and looking around the crowded bar. A hand landed on her shoulder. She turned to look, and a smile filled her face. She reached her arms out around his neck and gave him a kiss. "Byron! So good to see you. How has your trip been? Making any money?"

He stood smiling and holding his drink. "Hello Janine! Nah. Just having fun. Seeing shows, shopping, going to the power plant tomorrow for a tour. That kind of stuff." He saw me watching them and put out his hand. "Hi, I'm Byron. Are you a friend of Janine's here?"

What should I say? I was stuck.

Janine said, "You met Brook! This is my husband and soon to be bride."

His eyes popped open. My face flushed, and I lowered my head. He lifted my chin, smiling at me. "Way to go, girl. You're fabulous this way. Much more beautiful than last time we met. Congratulations! So, are you going to chop it off?"

"Uh...no way. I like that piece."

"Good!"

Janine took his hand. "I'm hoping she wants to get breasts and hips and such. I think she'll like that. We won ten thousand the other night and I've been thinking it could go toward that."

Byron looked me up and down. "She doesn't need it, but I'm sure she'd like it. Would you, Brook?"

I shrugged. "I haven't thought about it, but it sounds interesting." I bounced a foot, throbbing at the thought. That is something I could do. "Second thought. I thought about it and I want to. Good idea, Janine."

"Thanks."

Janine turned her chair and held Byron's arms while she pulled him closer and moved her leg between his to press on his cock. "Hmm, seems you like me or there's a zucchini in your pocket. Can us girls help you with that? We were just having a nightcap, and it's super you showed up. Like to go to our room?"

My heart raced. This was it. Janine was going to get fucked by a gorgeous black guy with a monumental cock. I told myself I was ready. Byron looked at me. "Brook? Is that okay with you? I'd love the company of two gorgeous women."

I nodded nervously. "Uh... sure. Really. Maybe one more drink though first?"

12

I was as buzzed as the plug buzzing in my bottom when Janine pulled back the covers to the satin sheets and Byron stripped all his clothes off revealing a silky smooth, firmly muscled, six foot three body with a flagpole standing before him as he looked at the two of us with a grin. "Is this okay, ladies?"

I dropped to my knees in reverence for that cock and used both hands and my mouth to devour it. Janine slid onto the bed and positioned herself to one side with her head on the pillow and her legs spread. She lowered her top and took out both her breasts and played with her clit while she watched me suck Byron. "You look so pretty with Byron's cock in your mouth, Brook. It looks so natural for you."

I nodded and mumbled around it. I wanted to make him come for me.

Janine watched quietly as I went after it with fervor, Byron's head rolling on his shoulders, then his hands holding my head as I looked up into his eyes.

Janine spoke up, "Don't make him come, sweetie. I want him to fuck me."

I wanted his come. I nodded and sped up more. Byron was moaning. I loved how he squeezed my head and looked into my eyes with those pretty brown eyes. I tugged his balls, stroked, gave it everything.

He pulled my head off and went to the bed. I scurried up onto my heels and by the time I made the bed; he was deep inside Janine, holding her knees pressed to the satin, her titanium high heels flailing in the air as he drove slowly and methodically into her. I slid onto the satin next to Janine and sucked her nipples. Her one hand slid down under my dress and grabbed my cock, wrapping it in the fluffy dress. She pulled my head to her. "Okay, sweetie. Same as the other night. I want you to come in your dress when he comes in me, okay?"

I nodded and rolled my head so I could watch that gorgeous, gleaming, wet, thick and solid chocolate cock with its thick urethra on the bottom side, and all its ripples of flesh and vein playing hide and seek in Janine. Her head rolled, and she moaned and squeaked, then slapped his hard ass and cried out, "Fuck me, Byron!! Please!... Stop torturing me and fuck me! Breed me and pump your come into me."

I had to stop humping into her hand and just let it rest in the nest of fluffy fabric she held it in. My plug in me had died, and no longer did any playlist. I knew Janine had hers in too and she wasn't going to take Byron in her bottom. No, my gorgeous wife was having a DP.

She held his ass with one hand, her nails digging in as he held her firm to the satin and rammed his drill into her stretched wet pussy. He grunted and shook the bed, making her head bob as their eyes locked on each other. Sweat gleamed on Byron's forehead and his legs stiffened behind him as he seemed to float above her bare, hard-nippled breasts.

All at once Janine's tiny body spasmed, and she squirted on him as he moaned a deep guttural moan and stuck it all the way, then pulled it out half way it and held it there. I watched as his cock swelled and pulsed and jerked and the fluid moved through it into my hot wife. I came in her hand instantly.

He fell to the other side of her, catching his breath, his long cock still curved into her leaking, oozing pussy. I dropped my head next to her, her hot breath on my face as she stroked my hair and whispered to me. "My lovely little girl. My love, my wife. You were so sweet." She kissed my head. I drifted off to sleep.

13

I woke to the bed shaking. Opening my eyes, I saw my wife on her back again in the same position she was when I last saw her. Byron's huge morning wood slowly gyrated in her while they kissed deeply. I slid over to her, wrapped a leg over hers, then slid my cock against her leg and humped it while I admired their coupling.

I saw then what she meant by having a man deep inside, coupling two bodies into one. Someday, I'd have to experience that filling by a real man, the way he moved inside her, how intensely she responded to it and how in love she was with it.

Her hand drifted down, and I moved up toward it, then she grasped my cock in my dress. She smiled and winked at me and I began humping into her silky, fluff filled hand while I stayed riveted on the show. Byron rotated his hips, slowly and deliberately permeating my wife's soul, in and back, in and back, his rigid cock bent slightly as it swirled and spread her. Janine shuddered, squirted and disposed of my cock and grabbed his hard ass with both hands.

I slid down to her leg and humped it like a puppy as she made Byron stop gyrating and just drive her bliss into her over and over, stretching her out and filling her to what appeared to be her throat. Breathily she told him, "Byron, my love, fuck me to heaven. Give me your passionate release. Fill me with your love."

Again, Byron grunted, moaned, locked eyes with her and his body stiffened as he shoved it in, then pulled it out halfway and let his come pump through his pulsing cock into my wife. The sight of my wife in a state of such connection to him and such passion for him made me come violently on her leg imagining being her.

I rolled to the side, grasped my cock in my dress, and fondled the last wonderful eruptions from it. Janine and Byron kissed deeply wrapped in an embrace, their hands roaming each other's bodies. After a couple of minutes of passionate, deep, heartfelt kissing, they went into the shower. I lay there spent, slowly fondling my cock in the fluff imagining how wonderful that must have been for her and whether I could ever feel such passion and love from another.

The more I imagined it, the quicker I stroked and I became hard as a rock again, my eyes closed, jerking my cock in my dress, my legs wrapped together, squeezing my package out and my breathing choppy as I whimpered quietly.

"Oh how adorable! Don"t let me interrupt you, princess." She kissed my cheek and my eyes popped open, my hand jerking my cock furiously. I stopped and stared at her, catching my breath. Byron smiled warmly at me.

Janine put my hand back on the front of my dress. "You don't have to stop, honey, while you shower, we'll go down and get some food and coffee and I'll pick up an outfit for you and we can all go to the power plant for the tours. Sound okay?"

"Yes honey. Sounds great."

The door slammed behind them. I had to get the monkey off my back and I had to relive my wife being fucked so well. Closing my eyes, I jerked in the fluff of my dress until I shook and whimpered again.

I stripped and put our dresses, bras, and panties in a laundry bag for dry cleaning and put it outside the door. I washed and hung our stockings, showered, did a light makeup, eyeshadow, mascara and lipstick and fluffed my hair. My new hair and makeup job made me proud. I felt confident in my skin, powerful. Feeling powerful and we're going to a power plant where power is generated. Interesting.

14

I sat in my robe at a small table with Janine, while she glowed radiantly. "Janine, you look so radiant today. Last night was good for you, huh?"

She rolled her eyes as she finished chewing. "Oh, my god. It's been so long... well, I have to say I don't think I ever had love made to me like that. Byron is *incredible*. He teases and controls my pleasure so well. He had me riding the edge of an orgasm forever and that cock of his seems to have an energy all its own. It's more like injecting my soul when he comes in me. Such power."

I nodded, feeling a little insecure.

"Don't worry, honey. It's you I love. You're my wife forever. As a matter of fact. When we stopped to pick up breakfast, I asked Byron if he'd like to make love to you, and it thrilled him. Would you enjoy that? I'd love to watch you two."

I nearly gagged on my orange juice. It was what I imagined. I longed for it, but it scared the hell out of me thinking of that huge cock in me. "Oh, my god. Janine. I don't know about that. I was so satisfied last night, and this morning on top of it, I don't have any desire for sex right now. I just want to feel feminine and pretty."

"Do you have your plug in? That might help with your libido."

"No. I just want to be a girl, not a nymphomaniac."

"Okay. That's fine. We'll just tour the power plant and have some fun and see where it goes. I bought you some padded undies and dress pants that will give you hips and butt and cover your front with a camel toe if they get pulled tight. You can wear them if you want. It'll be less sexual. Or you can wear a denim mini or something else."

"Pants sound good right now."

She stood and cleared the table. "Okay. Go get dressed and I'll clean up and we can go. We're supposed to meet him in about half an hour and Uber there."

I went into the bedroom where Janine had laid out my pants outfit. They were wide-leg cream-colored palazzo with slit sides and there was a matching, blousy, silky short sleeve, V-neck blouse and a pair of cream-colored open-toe high heels. Very classy.

I felt I should wear a pair of sheer pantyhose with them since my legs would be showing and I wanted them to look tan and silky. I slid the pantyhose on with the crotch cut out and then a pair of snug black panties and a matching bra. I slipped into the hip and butt makers, then the palazzo pants slid sensually over my legs and the padding on my hips and bottom gave me a lovely shape and seemed to be a part of me once on. I looked down at my crotch and there was no sign of my maleness and where the high waist of the palazzo pants sat, the crotch was tight enough to lightly show a camel toe as I walked.

I put on the blouse and tucked it in, then fastened the belt. I slipped into the high heels and went to the full-length mirror. It was wonderful. I slung my purse over my shoulder and filled it with my things. I put on my jewelry and sprayed perfume over my hair and blouse. The last thing I did was look in the mirror. Yes, I was much more powerful as a girl.

Janine and I went downstairs and met Byron in the lobby. His eyes lit up when he looked at me. Not us. Me. It made me feel self-conscious. "Hello ladies! What a glorious morning, isn't it? Brook, you look stunning and classy as hell. You'd probably look good in anything or nothing, but today you take my breath away." He took my hand, then leaned in for a kiss. I laughed and gave him a peck on his smooth, shaved cheek, his beautiful brown eyes bright and happy. At least my wife had very good taste. He was a hunk alright.

Our Uber arrived in a couple of minutes and we slid in the back together with Byron between us. His hand landed on my leg gently and slid on it while he gazed at me lovingly. I think Janine had set him a task, and he was full set to accomplish it. "You know Brook, the fact that you were a husband and now you're a wife is very exciting to me. It makes you very exotic. Not to mention courageous, alluring, and so powerful in the way you carry yourself and act. I don't know if it's your maleness making the power or your femaleness. You don't show any male aspects, yet you have tremendous gravitas."

My ego was getting bigger by the second. Now I see how compliments can carry a girl away. "Thank you so much. I feel much more powerful for sure. You made my day with your flattery."

I glanced at Janine, and she was smiling warmly at the two of us. I glanced at Byron's pants and could see the shadow of his semi hard cock. It throbbed when I glanced at it. He was hot for me, for sure. I throbbed in my panties beneath my camel toe. I placed my hand on his and slid it on my leg. My heart raced.

We arrived at the power plant and Byron ran off to buy tickets. Janine held my hand, and we walked slowly after Byron. "Seems Byron has an attraction to you, Brook."

"Seems he does."

"Are you okay with that?"

"He's nice. I love his flattery, of course. He is handsome and classy, for sure."

"Good. Then just relax and enjoy the day. I know you said you aren't feeling the least bit sexual today, anyway. But you let him caress your leg in the car. That's a good sign. Was that nice?"

I nodded. "His hand is so big and powerful!"

"Okay ladies! Here are our tickets."

We took them and thanked him. We all looked around for the entrance. Byron found it and took my hand in his huge mitt, gently tugging me forward with him. "There it is. Let's go ladies."

We walked hand in hand, his long strides slow and steady in pace with us so Janine and I could keep up in our shorter strides in moderate heels, clicking away across the pavement. My breasts jiggled beneath my blouse, tugging and showing my cleavage in the V-neck. My padded hips and butt seemed to be real as they swayed with each step. The fresh breeze blew through my hair, wafting the scent of Byron's cologne to me. His hand was soft and tender in guiding me along as we walked.

At the door, he moved forward, releasing my hand and opening it for us like the gentleman he was. He held it until we entered, then joined us again, taking my hand in his. Janine took my other hand in hers and whispered. "Such the gentleman. Enjoy it, there aren't that many around." She kissed my cheek and let my hand go as we passed through another doorway.

We came to the end of a line and stood waiting with the other visitors. Byron's big hands landed on my shoulders from behind and massaged them. He whispered in my ear. "Does this feel nice? I'm no masseuse, but maybe we should all get a massage today, too. I'll treat." He kissed my neck.

I shivered and laughed. "That tickled. Stop. You're such a tease, Byron."

"I *can't* stop. You're too powerful, buddy." He scrunched my shoulders with his fingers and I rolled my head, loving the feeling of his enormous hands on my shoulders. "Oh god, Byron. That feels lovely. Don't you think Janine would like that too? Why don't you give my wife one while we wait?"

He did the same for Janine. The two of them talking quietly and animatedly between them so I couldn't hear.

The line moved, and we went into a theater of sorts. A man was at a podium up front. Byron led us down the back row to the center, where we all sat with him to my right. His left arm slung itself over my shoulders and his hand clasped my shoulder, pulling me slightly to rest against his arm. His clean smelling cologne filled my nostrils.

"Is this okay, Brook?"

I put my hand on his firm thigh. My heart racing. "It's wonderful, actually." I gave him a peck on his cheek.

Janine patted my leg. "Good girl. Enjoy it." Then she caressed my leg.

We watched as the overview of the building of the plant and the final process of how the power from the water was transferred and moved, then turned into electricity. By the time it was over, I snuggled deliciously against Byron and felt relaxed and electric myself.

We stepped into a room where the power of the water rushing through the turbines made the floor shudder. The water was doing to the building what Byron had done to make my wife shudder from his power. The draw of gravity on the water was as impossible for it to resist as the turbines were to resist its entry to them or for them to generate their tremendous kilowatts. It was like two people being drawn together and feeling not only their power, but the power of their mate when the coupling occurred and their synergy created more power. I was throbbing in my panties while Byron held me close, his arm around me and Janine held my hand.

I squeezed his large, silky hand tight. "Oh my god, Byron. The power is incredible. I can feel it coursing through me."

He whispered in my ear. "And I can feel your feminine power teasing me with its strength and beauty." His arm around me, he rubbed my arm and held me tight. He leaned way down to peer into my eyes, so I met his big, light brown, glittering eyes. He brought his lips to mine and ever so gently kissed my lips, his tongue slipping past my teeth to bring me spearmint flavor as our tongues danced and my head became dizzy.

I held onto him to keep from falling. I pulled away gently and gazed into his eyes. "Oh, my.... What got into me? You make my head spin."

"I'm sorry, Brook. Are you okay? Do you need me to carry you?" He held both my hands, then felt my forehead, moving my bangs aside. "Are you okay, my dear?"

"Oh god yes. I'm very okay. It was just that epiphany about power and connectedness and then... then we kissed and it seemed ... seemed... intoxicating. I felt so powerful and you felt so powerful."

"Let me be your water, miss turbine. I need to finish my journey with you."

"Oh god. Yes, and I need to be filled with your power."

Janine stood there waiting. I turned to see her loving eyes on us. "I think you're ready young lady."

15

We Ubered back to the hotels, the three of us discussing my epiphany, and the more we talked about it, the more I realized I had never felt power as a male and now as a woman, I feel more power coming and going from me than I ever knew could happen.

Janine kissed my cheek. "That's wonderful. See? This was for you. I knew you would find your true power. I knew it. I'm so proud of you. Now all we need is those dresses and you can be a bride."

Byron lifted an eye. "I thought you two were married already."

Janine nodded. "We were. But Brook has this thing about being a bride. That's how this all started was with my wedding dress. It captivated her and now she has her own on order. Now all we need is to do a wedding ceremony again."

"Ah... I see. So you'll get married as two wives."

"Yes, but we'll need grooms to bring the power to it that a typical bride would feel. Brook needs to have a man stand by her side next time. Just for the ceremony and the consummation. I mean, we'd still be married, but she'd get to fully experience being a bride. That's the key."

Byron, his arm around me, took his other hand and turned my head to him by his cheek. "Can I be your husband for the wedding?"

I looked at Janine. "But what about you, Janine?"

"I can find a guy to be my groom, I think."

Byron said, "You know, I flew out here with a bunch of guys. I'll bet they'd like to meet you two tonight and then they'd probably be fighting over who could play the role of husband."

Janine's eyes opened wide. "Really? You have friends out here? Are they as classy and gentlemanly and open-minded as you?"

"Very much so."

Janine looked at me. "Want to meet Byron's friends tonight?"

"Absolutely. Sounds great!"

Back at the hotel, they told us we had a delivery that was put in the room.

"Your dress!" Janine grabbed my hand and tugged us to the elevator.

Byron chased behind. "Wait! What time, where? What's the plan, ladies?"

I turned to him, taking control and feeling my power. "Dinner at six at Bellagio. Wedding at 9 at the Elvis Drag Queen Chapel. Consummation in our room thereafter. Bring all your friends and have them dress for a wedding as if they were the grooms. Janine and I will be their brides tonight. Right Janine?"

She grinned ear to ear. "Oh yes. Both of us in our wedding dresses. Tell them to be ready to satisfy us."

16

I booked a private room at Bellagio for drinks and dinner, along with a ride in a limo from our hotel to the Bellagio, even though we could have walked. The dress had indeed arrived and was a perfect fit. I was beside myself with emotions and excitement, filled with energy and frantic to get it all right. We still had hours to go and everything was ready. My heart was racing.

Janine wrapped an arm around me as I stood looking at my wedding things on the bed next to my wedding dress. "Settle down, princess. It's normal to be nervous about your wedding night, but you need to calm down. Why don't we go for a massage, mud-bath exfoliation, and coconut oil bath like we did the first day. It'll increase your sensuality and relax you."

I took a deep breath and remembered it. "That was heavenly." I looked at my watch. "We do have plenty of time. Let's do it. I need the diversion."

I changed out of my pants and restricting padded underpants and took Janine's advice and inserted my happy-butt plug like she did and turned it on. I slipped into a flowing floral layered cotton minidress like Janine's, where I could be free in crotchless panties and feel the air on my bare skin. Wedge heels completed my new liberating outfit and off we went, feeling as aroused as I had ever been.

The massage was just as incredible, the lovely masseuse bringing me to the edge over and over and pressing on my plug, driving me to push against it. The mud bath was a thorough exfoliation of every body part and I mean every one, including my fingers, toes, palms, and as much as it could be without making it spurt, my cock.

Next was the warm, scented, coconut oil bath, leaving my skin tingly and utterly silky smooth. Every cell of my skin could now feel every nuance of touch and fabric, delighting me and sending ripples of pleasure throughout. It was filling me with power.

We walked back to the room, my cock flailing delightfully in the breeze under my dress with each step, my breasts tugging on my chest. I held my head high, feeling my power and knowing how alluring and desirable I truly was. And now, I was to be a bride!

Back in the room, Janine helped me to do my hair, curling it with an iron and setting the look with spray. She helped with my makeup as we both turned ourselves into blushing brides.

We dressed in the bedroom together, each of us slipping into our sheer white gartered stockings and garter belts with baby blue garters at the tops of the stockings and a baby blue garter wrapped around my silky globes and hard cock, lifting it and helping it stay proud beneath the fluffy, soft layers of the short front of the dress. The dress itself held my breast-forms tight and lifted, making luscious cleavage after Janine and I took turns tying our corseted backs of the dresses snug.

The bridal veils locked into our hair nicely, draping across our shoulders when in back and across our faces when the front piece was lowered. The fetishy high, white strappy stilettos made us walk in tiny minced and vulnerable steps and our crotchless panties made us totally vulnerable beneath. We slid on our long, white, fingerless stretch-lace gloves, accenting our rings and painted long nails. I was in a second heaven as I paced the floor, being sure my jewelry was right and my lipstick perfect and my purse not missing anything.

We stood before the mirror admiring each other. "Look at you, missy! You're a bride!" She kissed my cheek gently. "I love seeing what used to be my husband in *his wedding dress*."

I wrapped my arms around her and gave her a hug. "And I love becoming a bride. I love you so much."

Janine lifted the front of her dress and hiked up one leg, grasping my cock and slipping it into her. "Mmm, you're so cute. Now no coming yet."

My heart raced, and I withdrew from her. "Sorry. You still have that effect."

She laughed. "No problem, sister. I'll have plenty. The grooms will breed your wife many times."

She went into the bathroom and came out with a damp washcloth and knelt before me and gently washed my cock and balls, then took her twenty-four-hour lipstick and painted the tip of my cock bright metallic pink like her lipstick. She blew on it until it dried, then put another coat on. "There! A feminine cock. It looks lovely on a girl like you."

I stared down at it as it leapt and fell in the cool air. It was feminine and pretty. I loved it. "Thank you. It is pretty now. Good idea."

"Of course." She handed me a pill. "Take this. Even if you come, you'll still stay hard and it'll feel good. You may even come more than once, given a little time and stimulation."

I popped it on my tongue and swallowed it.

"Ready to be a bride wearing her wedding dress?" She looked at her watch. "The boys should be downstairs in the bar waiting for us, and the limo is out front."

"God, am I ready? I'm so glad you caught me wearing your dress now." I gave her a kiss on the lips and took her hand. "Let's go find our husbands."

17

Our wedding party awaited. They were all as handsome and nice as Byron. Some white, some black, all looking the part of a groom. Six handsome men and two brides. What a fantastic wedding this promised to be.

We piled into the Limo, Byron's arm slid around me. Another guy poured champagne. The driver took the liberty to take us for a leisurely drive until we finished the champagne and I could suck Byron's cock and tease another one with my hand while Janie sucked and stroked the others. We exited the limo, all the men hard, and took the time to let everyone calm down and have a smoke before going in. I held my flower bouquet that the boys bought us like Janine's in my hand with my purse and held Byron's hand before entering. The people in the entry greeted us with hoots, howls, and congratulations.

The manager showed us our private room, complete with dining table for eight, bar, and multiple couches, all in the classy Bellagio style. We all got drinks and began milling about getting to know the men. Of course, Byron was especially careful to stay close, and he was full of flattery for me as his bride.

I sat on the couch, and Byron sat next to me. Another handsome, tall, black man named Brice sat on the other side of me and then a cute and adorable, boyish guy about my size named Pat stood before us.

Pat smiled at me, his eyes flitting about, checking out my legs and cleavage, then back to my eyes and hair and lips. "Soo, you're going to be a bride for *all* of us?"

I nodded. "Pretty neat, huh?"

He raised his eyebrows. "It sure is. Thanks for having us."

I slid my hand over Byron's and Brice's crotches, gratified by their hard cocks in their pants. I smiled at them both. "Maybe you men could oblige me by taking out your manhoods? Pat, could you as well?"

They all unzipped and removed their shaved globes and cocks. Byron's was by far the largest. Brice's was smaller but still substantial and Pat had an adorable one, which he held and stroked with a thumb and a forefinger. "Bring me that, Pat. It's so cute."

He moved between my legs and I grasped it between my thumb and forefinger with one hand, then cradled his balls in my white lace covered palm and rolled them. I flicked the tip with my tongue, then took it into my mouth and bobbed my head on it, squeezing it with my puckered lips and looking up into his pretty eyes.

Pat whimpered and gently laid his hand on my head. Instantly, he gave a little squeal and his legs tensed and his cock pulsed in my mouth, complimenting me with the sweetest tasting come I could have ever imagined while he gazed lovingly into my eyes.

When he finished twitching and shooting, I cleaned his cock thoroughly with my tongue, making him shudder, then he took it away from me and hid it back in his pants. "Oh gosh. That was fantastic, ma'am. Thank you."

"You're very welcome, Pat. Have you ever thought about presenting as a girl?"

"Yes, ma'am. I'd like to try that some day."

"We'll have to stay in touch. Now make sure you're hard later. I want more of that adorable cock. Okay, princess?"

"Princess. I like that. I'll be ready."

He left to go get a drink. Byron handed me mine, and I drank it down, then gave the glass back to him to put on the end table. Janine was playing with her grooms on another couch and appeared to be having a good time. The next fifteen minutes or so, I spent going back and forth between Byron and Brice, sucking their lovely chocolate cocks bringing them to the edge, but not letting them come. Brice was getting a little upset with me. "Damn you, wife. Let me come in your face. I'll be ready again in no time."

"It's *my* day, Brice. I get to decide when and where my groom comes. I'm the Bride, remember?"

Byron laughed. "She's right, Brice. Hang in there and let her torture you. You'll get off soon enough."

Brice grumbled as I went back to Byron and used both hands and my mouth to indulge in his fabulous maleness.

Needless to say, my cock was doing jigs and oozing under my dress in the fluffy fabric all the time. A knock came on the door. No one changed what they were doing except Pat, who opened it.

A formally attired waiter stood smiling with a towel across one arm while he took in the sights. He spoke to Pat, "I can bring in appetizers if you're ready for them. I was told you all needed to be at the chapel at nine. It's now seven thirty."

Janine sat up and wiped her lips, then smiled at him. "Please, come here, Pat, you too, sir."

The waiter was hard in his pants. All the other guys except Pat had their cocks out, gleaming and wet while they stroked them. I was stroking Byron, wondering what Janine was up to.

"So, sir, we'd like appetizers soon, but maybe before you go to get them, you'd like to offer yourself as an appetizer to a fine pair of lips."

His eyes lit up, and a grin crossed his face as his cock danced in his pants. "Sure. That sounds fantastic."

"Okay, close your eyes."

Janine stood and whispered to Pat. "I heard you say you'd like to present as a girl someday. Why not see if you pass the cock sucking test with the waiter?"

Pat's pretty eyes went wide, and he covered his mouth and held back a giggle, nodding excitedly.

She turned to the waiter. "Now don't open your eyes."

"I won't, I promise, ma'am."

She went over to him, took the towel from his arm, and tied it as a blindfold for him. "There. Now leave that on."

"Yes ma'am."

Adorable Pat nodded and smiled ear to ear. He knelt before the waiter, unzipped the waiter's pants, took his cock out, and fervently sucked it for him. You could see the passion Pat had for it and he didn't take long to get his reward from the waiter who grunted and moaned while fucking Pat's face and filling it with come. He tucked himself away.

Pat stood and composed himself, and Janine took the waiter's blindfold off. "The waiter smiled at Janine. "Thanks. That was fantastic. Not sure what the blindfold was for, but it was still great. Best I ever had. You're one hell of a woman."

Janine giggled and nodded and said, "Thank you. Okay, you can bring in the appetizers now."

He left.

Pat got pats on the back and encouragement from the others to present as a woman. "He said I passed as one hell of a woman. I guess I have to live up to it soon." He giggled.

We all put ourselves in order and just enjoyed appetizers and drinks like normal people. All the while, I was bobbing under my dress, dying to get fucked. Janine and I sat snuggled together on the couch caressing each other's sheer white stockinged legs unconsciously while she told stories of us to Pat and how she determined I would be happier as a woman.

We ate dinner together. Pat practiced her skills on the men under the table from one to the other after she hurriedly consumed her meal and asked permission to go below, promising not to let any man come. Pat skipped desert and kept the men on the edge.

After espresso, it was time to hop in the Limo and go to the Chapel, which we did.

A tall, gorgeous queen with a woman acting like a feminine Elvis alongside (if you can imagine that) Stood before us, Janine next to me and our grooms lined up on each side.

"My goodness. Too bad this isn't for real girls. You have three each of the hottest guys on the planet. Now. For the words."

"Do you Janine take Michael, Gabriel, and Bob to be your husbands to fuck you whenever they want to and honor you with cock and breed you like their slut?"

Janine chortled. "I do."

They all replied, "We do."

"Very well. Now Brook. Do you Brook take Byron, Brice, and Pat to be your husbands to fuck you whenever they want to and honor you with cock and breed you like their slut?"

My heart raced. My cock leapt. "Oh god yes. Please."

"Do you men take Brook to be your bride to fuck until she's silly and to receive your come in anyplace you want to put it on or in her anytime you want to?"

"We do."

"Then ladies and gentlemen. I pronounce you men and wives. Go breed your brides, gentlemen."

Byron lifted me under my knees, and I wrapped my arm around his neck. They picked up Janine as well and they carried us to the Limo.

18

Janine wasted no time pulling back the covers and sliding onto the satin sheets, her legs back, firm, hard-nippled boobs out of her dress, with her face glowing like the bride she was, waiting to be bred.

Michael stripped, lubed his cock, and slid over to her, grabbing her by the waist and lifting her while holding his thick, long cock and guiding it into her tight bottom bit by bit until she could sit on his thighs. She laid back and Gabriel slid on top of her guiding his cock between the white ruffles of her crotchless panties while he pressed her legs back, her feet in her fetishy high heels back by her ears and he pressed his cock slowly into her, stretching her out. Her eyes went wide, and she glanced at me and winked.

Gabriel fucked her slowly and deliberately, gyrating his hips and using the full length of his cock in her. Her eyes rolled in her head, then she locked eyes with him as she fondled her breasts and Michael and Brice took turns diving their cock into my wife, both men grunting and moaning.

Janine whimpered then said in a choppy voice, "Fuck yeah husbands. Fuck your slut wife."

Bob came around to her side and turned her head toward him. Her mouth opened instinctively and his cock went into her face, his hands tight on her head, then he fucked my wife's face.

They all got into a rhythm, and I finally gave my attention to *my* husbands as their wife. All of my men were naked. I lubed Byron's enormous cock, making it shine and gleam as a drop oozed from the fat head. I took Byron by the hand and I slid onto the bed. He slid between my legs and held them back with his thick hands on my thighs, my heels in the air above my head. He guided his missile toward me, pressing the thick head against my hole and I pushed against it, stretching myself.

We pushed together over and over, getting it a little deeper into me each time until finally it made it past the gate and I gasped with pleasure.

"Are you okay, Brook?"

"I'm in heaven. Breed me, my husband."

Byron slid it slowly in and out of me until it was able to completely hide in my ass. I watched it below my bobbing cock, the white silky fluff of my wedding dress between us.

"Oh god yes, Byron. How do I feel, honey?"

"Fabulous. Like a virgin bride." His eyes looked into mine lovingly.

"That's because you're the first. Make love to me." I looked around while Byron began gyrating his hips in circles and thrusting, sending ripples of pleasure through me and making my flailing cock ooze. Brice and Pat stood there jerking their cocks, watching. I called Pat over and had him lie alongside of me and I lowered my hand to his cock and grasped it so he could hump into my hand.

Brice I called to the side and opened my mouth for him to fill it with his cock, which he did, and held my head tight to fuck my face, my lips puckered and tight on his silky, rigid rod.

Pat humped my hand, Brice fucked my face, Byron sent his passion rippling into my soul and this went on for what seemed days as I drifted into some alternate space where there was only cock skin all over my body and lips, and every sensation I received was just more love being made to me. They filled me with power and grace, allure, and femininity. My gorgeous husbands lusted for me on my wedding night, ravaging their bride.

I lay there, seeing Byron in all his beastly glory while sucking Brice's cock and feeling Pat's adorable hard cock on my silky gloved palm. My wife lay next to me being bred in her bottom, in front, and in her face, moaning, shuddering, squirting, and whimpering as if she was being whipped, though I knew those were sounds of overwhelming pleasure, not pain because I was doing the same.

Brice's hand squeezed my head tight, and he stopped fucking my face for a moment until the first gush shot across my tongue and then he held my head tight and fucked it fast. I swallowed his thick voluminous spunk greedily until there was no more, then tried to run my tongue in circles around it to coax more out. He pulled it from my face as he whispered, stop honey, stop."

I was now free to gaze upon Pat humping my hand, hugging me and squeezing my breasts while she whimpered alongside. I looked down at my cock flailing in its wrapping of a baby-blue garter with drips flying off the tip. Byron's cock slid in and out of me and I looked into his eyes and said, "Fuck me, husband. Fuck your bride and breed her. Come inside of her." I squeezed Pat's cock in my gloved hand. "Pat, come in my hand, young lady, when Byron comes in me." She whimpered and snuggled.

Janine called out next to me. "Yes, Michael and Gabriel, you too. Come in me when Byron comes." Bob had already come in my wife's face and was diligently trying to jerk his cock hard while standing to the side.

Byron had the power no to control now of all of our finishes. He took his sweet time, being sure to torture us all for a good while. Bob was hard again and by Janine's face, looking down at her while she locked her eyes on Gabriel's. "Fuck me husband. Fuck your bride. Come with me when Byron comes. You too, Michael!"

Michael held her hips and moved his cock in and out of her bottom the best he could while Gabriel fucked her like an animal and Bob jerked his cock in her hair and veil.

Byron draped my veil over my face reminding me of the bride I was and making me look through it like a mist, into his eyes. He finally drew his cock out of me almost all the way. He grunted. "Here it is, honey!" He shoved it deep and held it there, his eyes locked on mine through the veil. It swelled and pulsed in me. Pat's cock spewed his seed into my silky gloved palm, Bob shot ropes over and into Janine's hair, Gabriel went rigid shoving his cock into my wife and filled her pussy with come to ooze around his cock while Michael's cock pulsed in her bottom dumping his load into her sweet bottom.

After a bunch of moaning and grunting from the men, whimpering from Janine, Pat and me, everything went silent except for the sound of deep breathing. Byron let my legs go, and they slid down. He slid to the side Pat wasn't on, his cock still partly in me. He peppered my face with kisses.

Pat put a leg over my sheer stockinged leg and pressed his adorable damp cock against it, slipping it deliciously over it. Brice leaned his cock over my face, lowered my jaw with his finger and shot his come into it. I swished it around in my mouth and savored the reward until I couldn't resist swallowing it.

We lay there spent for a while, then the men moved about and dressed. I snuggled Pat against me, still pressing her now hardening cock against my stockinged leg. I caressed her hair.

Byron kissed my cheek. Good night, lovely bride. I don't think we'd be comfortable, all of us sleeping in one bed. The others said their goodbyes to me and Janine.

Byron slapped Pat's bare bottom. "Coming Pat?"

"Can I stay? If it's okay with Janine and Brook?"

Janine spoke up. "Of course you can. Right Brook?"

"Of course."

Janine said, "Okay Byron? We'll deliver her tomorrow, dressed the way she should be. Okay?"

"If Pat's okay with that. We are, right, guys?"

Brice said to the group, "Absolutely. We'd love to see our little buddy all done up properly, like the girl she is." They all nodded.

Pat said, smiling ear to ear, "I can't wait. Thank you two so much!"

"Lets get you some nice night clothes then and we can get some rest, okay?" I slid off the bed and put my hand out to her.

19

Everyone except Pat left us. We dressed her in a cute negligee and thigh-high stockings and she wanted to wear high heels and, as it turned out, she fit in mine, so I let her wear them to bed. Janine and I wore our nightclothes and stockings and we all slid under the satin sheets and snuggled.

Pat was hard again and tossing and turning and finally ended up snuggled against me, slipping her cock on my stockinged leg. I took her soft hand, put it on my cock, and she stroked me.

Janine interrupted us and slid between us. "Okay ladies. Suck my tits." We each took one and Janine played with her clit a bit, then she gave us each a hand with a pair of panties in each and grasped our cocks. "Okay girls. We need to sleep. Hump these panties and let's go to sleep."

We humped, we whimpered, and we held tight to Janine while we sucked her nipples and we both came together, then we all fell fast asleep.

20

We slept like queens. We showered together and took Pat to the salon and had her hair and nails done. We bought her a pretty flowered minidress and heels, breast forms, stockings and all the things she needed to start being the girl she was. Then we met up with her buddies, our husbands, from last night.

They were more than excited to see Pat all redone and Pat was like she found a new place in the world where she could be special to her favorite guys that had always taken care of her when others saw her as nothing more than a geeky boy to pick on.

She stood next to Byron beaming, his arm holding her close, and she said to us, "Thank you for taking care of me and helping me become who I am. Now, maybe, if they'll let me, I can give some pleasure to my best friends who always took such good care of me."

Janine and I nodded and Janine said, "No thanks needed. See how all these things can work out? Just like my wife Brook and I. She wrapped her arm around me. Now we're free. Right Brook? Were you the least bit jealous of me with the men?"

"Nope. Not a bit."

"Nor I of you. The world is *filled* with abundance. Some people think that if they don't have something, it's because others have it and there isn't enough to go around, so they need to hoard it, whether that's a lover or money or whatever. Once everyone realizes there's enough for everyone, greed, jealousy, it all goes away and we're left with love and life like we have here."

The men nodded. Pat asked, "So how long are you two here for and what plans do you have? If I may ask. We have to leave in the morning."

"We have a couple more weeks. Plans? Just to relax and enjoy our new relationship and lives. You?"

She hugged Byron next to her. "I want to make it up to my best friends here and take care of them for a change. Maybe we can get together?"

"Let's do it. We'll exchange numbers, all of us," I said. "How about after the honeymoon for us and the vacation for you?"

Pat smiled. "I have some other geek friends that I want to show a new way to live and maybe help them achieve this wonderful new world." She curtsied with her dress and giggled. "Wanna help?"

I laughed. "That's funny. I had the same thought about what to do when we went home. Maybe we can all start a club and expand this. Maybe we can raise money and make more special girls."

Byron smiled ear to ear. "Wow. Okay, ladies. Now that Janine's husband has worn *his wedding dress*, I guess we all have our plans. Now let's go forward into life. I'm buying lunch."

If you enjoyed this book, it would be great if you could leave a review and tell a friend about it or blog it out. Thanks!

Barb and Thom

For more of our books, both fiction and non-fiction, in Kindle, paperback and Audible versions, go to:

Amazon:

http://www.amazon.com/Barbara-Deloto/e/B00J21HWA4/